I'm Okay,
You're Dead

I'm Okay, You're Dead

A Harbour Pointe Mystery

I'm Okay, You're Dead

Joyce Spizer

INTERCONTINENTAL PUBLISHING

ISBN 1 881164 85 3

1st American edition: 2000

Typography: Monica Rozier
Cover by: Raul Melendez

Library of Congress Cataloging-in-Publication Data

Spizer, Joyce
    I'm okay you're dead / Joyce Spizer.--1st American ed.
        p.   cm.
    ISBN 1-881164-85-3 (alk. paper)
1.   Private investigators–Fiction.   I. Title.
    PS3569.P59   I4 2000
    813'.54–dc21   00-009458
                                                                CIP

Acknowledgments

Always thanks to cousin *John Blackburn*, the real Johnnie Blake, who conveniently dislocated his arm giving me the idea to have him shot. He asked, "Will it hurt much?" I love you John.

Cindy Fields and her wonderful family, *John*, *Tanya* and *John Jr.* Cindy, the daughter I always wanted, who entered my life at the perfect time.

A special thanks to Raul Melendez, author of *Mercy Street*, a friend whose generosity of time and creativity led not only to development and maintenance of my Website, but for the magnificent graphics that grace the dust jacket of this novel. I'm thrilled to hold the position of mentor.

Back in my life after an absence of too many years, I welcome *Ann Fears Crawford Ph.D.*, a fellow author, my high school teacher, and dear friend.

To *Roberta Rey*, a creative spirit in my life, who kept decorating our home long after I left the room. A new and forever friend.

George, Vivian, Jake and *Fluffy Jaggard* whose encouragement, friendship, and humor keeps me going.

Jan McGaff, formerly of the LAPD, who described being shot in more detail than anyone should ever need to know.

To new friends, Claude Rogers, Jr., and his beautiful wife Bernadine, who spent another year of their lives defending accused serial killer and brother, Glen Rogers. Thank you for your patience, trust, and confidence as your story, *The Glen Rogers Story, The Cross Country Killer*, now takes shape.

DeAnn Lubell, the President of National League of American Pen Women, Palm Springs Branch, who is much more than that. Such a generous sweet soul.

To Barbara McClure, editor of *Desert Woman*, a dear friend with a fine edit pen.

To wonderful and supportive writer friends, *Gerald Schiller, Taylor Smith, Earlene Fowler, Maxine O'Callaghan, Barbara Seranella, Rochelle Krich, Marisa Babjak-Wiggins*, and, of course, always . . . *Sue Grafton* and *Ray Bradbury*.

Shannon Friedman and *Dr. Judith Zacher*, who openly discussed plastic surgery procedures with me.

James Camp, Deputy Coroner for Riverside County, who I found quite by coincidence. Jim, a fellow Sweetwater, Texan, whose great laughter and cooperative spirit will make us steadfast friends. Look for his debut novel.

Los Angeles FBI Special Agent, *John Hoos*, who gave me honest answers and great advice. Any procedural mistakes infused into this novel are mine and mine alone.

Alan Nestlinger with Orange County Flood Control, who never questioned my reasons when I opened our conversation, "Suppose I wanted to toss a dead body . . ."

Tony and *Dina Shawkat* and their gorgeous staff at "Show Girls," a Gentlemen's Club, where beauty is more than skin deep.

And most of all to Sisters-in-Crime (Orange County, Los Angeles, San Luis Obispo, Fresno, and all the Texas Chapters), NLAPW, NWA, PWLLB, MWA, Private Eyes of America, Round Table West, and ICWA, always flying "Hurrah" banners for the successes of their members on tour.

Dedicated entirely to
My Beloved Husband,
Harold.
Whose first year of "retirement" was spent
Driving me on the by-ways and highways of America
Promoting The Cop was White as Snow

—Three may keep a secret, if two of them are dead.
Benjamin Franklin, 1706-1790
Poor Richard's Almanac, July 1735

❖ Chapter 1 ❖

Camellia "Mel" Walker tightened the grip on her purse as two young men, using hand signals and wearing gang colors, approached her.

"Damn," Mel mumbled to herself. "I'm back in Los Angeles, the city of grime, crime, and scum, and me without a gun."

Weary after a five-hour plane ride and a three-hour time change, Mel stretched her five-foot, six-inch frame, and pulled the raincoat close around her trim body. She paced the length of one of LAX's covered walkways, suitcase in hand, dodging a tidal wave of humanity that swirled around her on its way to catch any number of planes.

Despite the staccato drumming of a torrential downpour outside, infused with rumbles of thunder and flashes of lightning, Mel could not miss Johnnie Blake's more dramatic arrival. The horn of his 1968 pumpkin-colored Mustang blared through the din of airport activity as he swerved from lane to lane, like a race car vying for position, before skidding to a stop, and double-parking near her.

Johnnie bounced from the car and maneuvered around the herds of travelers and their luggage. He grimaced as he reached Mel.

"My God. What we need today is a boat." Johnnie's voice gave the gentlest hint as to his sexuality.

She hugged him. "You got that right."

9

He grabbed her bags and they dashed for the Mustang.

"So, how was Maui?"

"Warm, sunny, and refreshing. And not nearly long enough."

He squeezed her hand. "I'm sure happy you're back. Business is hopping."

Business involved grime, crime, and scum. She called the company Walker Investigations.

Mel smiled, "That's great news."

Inside, the car was warm and the windshield wiper blades made squeaking noises on every down motion. She laid her head against the seat and twirled strands of brown hair between her fingers, a soothing trait from childhood. Johnnie gripped the steering wheel as rain pummeled the Mustang, running rivers down the windows.

Mel watched Johnnie as he navigated around reckless drivers. His baby-fine hair was neatly brushed and rubber-banded at the nape of his neck. A two-day growth of stubble pushed past slightly pockmarked cheeks.

Johnnie had answered an ad she placed in the newspaper. Walker Investigations overflowed with work at a time when Mel ricocheted from her son Willie's death and her subsequent divorce from Taylor Lawrence Archer. Johnnie's specialty, death penalty cases, segued perfectly with her criminal and civil background. The fact that he was a proud gay man enhanced his innate charm. After her dad died, the renovated family home became the office of Walker Investigations. Johnnie had taken up residence in the garage apartment behind the office.

Johnnie broke the silence. "You don't have much of a tan."

"Oh, I'm not much of a sun goddess. I caught up on my reading though."

"Meet anyone interesting?"

"Wasn't looking, I guess." With one finger, she traced the rain pellets that ran in rivulets down the door window.

"That means Patty Dotson's cousin didn't join you. Did he at least call?"

"Lucas Tanner? He wanted to fly over. But he's got some oil deal working. Near Africa, I think. He called me several times. We had nice long talks."

"Phone calls aren't very good pillow companions."

"No, they aren't. I miss him more than I thought I would."

Mel met Lucas at Patty's boat parade party the previous Christmas. Between her California home and career and his Texas home and his worldwide career in oil exploration, their time together had been exciting but limited.

"That's the first time I heard you admit it."

"I'm too vulnerable right now. Let's shelve this Lucas topic for now. Is there anything I should know about?"

Johnnie reached behind her, picked up a crudely addressed envelope, and plopped it in her lap. "This came today."

Mel used the end of a ballpoint pen to slit one end of the envelope. She withdrew a piece of red-and-cream-colored paper and a handwritten note. She read the note aloud: "I need your help and can't go the police. They wouldn't believe me anyway. Here is part of your fee. If you're interested in getting the balance, meet me at seven o'clock Tuesday, behind *La Casa*."

Johnnie glanced at Mel. She turned the envelope over.

"No return address."

"It's postmarked Newport Beach." Johnnie kept his eyes on the road as he spoke. Oncoming traffic splashed sheets of water across the car's hood. "What's clipped to the note?"

"It looks like part of a bond of some kind. Hmm. Worth ten thousand dollars. What's today?"

"Tuesday."

She glanced at her watch, pulled out the stem, then asked, "I'm confused. What's the time here?"

"Six-thirty."

"Let's go. How hard can collecting this fee be?"

The rain continued to pound the car throughout the gloomy drive. The wipers labored as oil and grease boiled up from the highways, making Johnnie's drive to *La Casa* precarious. The smell of ozone, damp and acrid, filled the air.

Parked cars occupied every available space at the popular *La Casa* Restaurant. A young couple left a nearby bar and stood under an awning. Water cascaded down on them from all sides of the faded blue canvas.

"My luck," Mel said, pointing to the couple. "Double park here for a minute. That looks promising."

Johnnie did as instructed.

The man removed his suit jacket and held it over the woman's head. After a few moments, Johnnie backed his Mustang into the vacated spot at the curb.

Mel snatched a flashlight off the back seat, buttoned her raincoat, and took one deep breath as she and Johnnie stepped into the alley behind *La Casa*. Her hand shook as she cast the light over the weeping brick walls that leaned oppressively toward her.

"I should have brought my gun," she said.

The stench of overripe garbage assailed her. A gray, gooey substance, smelling like tar and decay, dripped down one wall.

Johnnie put his hand out to halt Mel's progress. They listened. Behind them, far away it seemed, were the noises of the city. Here, Mel felt only her beating heart and heard the scampering of small animals. She held her breath and hearing nothing, edged forward into the darkness.

A single light was mounted above a faded wooden sign that spelled out *La Casa*. The door had long since given up its white paint to the elements. Mel turned off the flashlight, stuffed it into her coat pocket, and waited.

Footsteps approached from the depths of the alley. Then a masculine, smoker's voice, spoke, "Who's that with you?"

"My associate, Mr. Blake."

"I hope you've decided to take my case." The figure hovered in the shadows and coughed deep, wet, and raspy.

"We'd like to hear more about it, but I'm sure we can, Mister … you know this isn't the best place to discuss your case." Mel took a step forward. "How about some coffee? There's a place …"

"No," the man interrupted. "This is fine. I don't have much time."

"Are you sure the police wouldn't like to know about this?" Johnnie asked.

"No. Absolutely not. Now, I have money. A lot of it. Only it's missing. And I'm willing to pay you ten thousand dollars to find it."

Rain poured down Mel's neck, drenching the clothes beneath her coat.

She heard rapid footsteps tapping closer in the darkness. As if on cue, the light over *La Casa's* door faded. A shot rang out, echoing through the alley's hollowness between the walls.

Mel dropped to the ground and remained still. Several rats frantically dashed toward her, splashing through puddles of water. She heard a thud followed by silence.

"Are you okay?" was the only thing Mel could think to say.

A new voice, a deep baritone replied, "I'm okay. You're dead."

Then two more shots rang out.

❖ Chapter 2 ❖

Mel heard the gunshots, a high-pitched scream, and a splashing thud near her. She hugged the wet gooey asphalt of the alley with her body and remained motionless. Maybe the assailant will believe the bullets found their mark, she thought.

Heavy footsteps faded into the darkness ahead of her. For a moment all she could hear was the patter of rain. Near her, to her left, she heard a moaning, "Mel, I'm hit. Oh, it burns so bad." And from farther away she heard a gurgle, like oil bubbling out of the ground.

She felt no pain, but got to her knees and rubbed her hands over her upper body checking for entry wounds.

"Mel, help me."

She pulled the flashlight from her pocket and scrambled on hands and knees to Johnnie's body. He clutched his bloody right arm. Johnnie's knees were drawn into a fetal position. His hazel eyes crinkled in pain and were wild with fear. "Am I gonna die?"

Mel moved the light over his body looking for other wounds.

15

"No, you're not going to die. But that's going to hurt like hell tomorrow morning."

"Oh, shit, it burns like hell tonight."

She laid the flashlight on the pavement facing Johnnie and withdrew a scarf from a raincoat pocket.

Johnnie winced as she wrapped the scarf tightly around the arm above the bloody area of his coat, twisting the kerchief tightly into a tourniquet.

She patted him lightly. "Don't move now. I'll check on our client."

Mel scrambled to her feet and walked toward their client. She shined the light back and forth across the alley until she found tennis shoes, not a name brand, well-worn, white, crew-socks with elastic bands unraveling. The light traced a pair of brown wash-slacks and a tan flannel shirt, to a slim body and a small, neatly trimmed mustache with a matching thinning head of black hair that floated in a pool of blood. Square in the center of the forehead was a tiny exit wound.

She touched the man's jawline. No pulse. The gurgling stopped.

The sounds of siren blasts startled Mel to her feet and she ran past Johnnie to the street. "Shit. X-Ray is gonna love this."

"Think how I feel," Johnnie called after her.

Mel's mind raced as first one, then a second black-and-white police car screeched to a halt in the middle of the street, partially blocking the alley. Both cars faced headlight-to-headlight catching her in their beams.

Now I know what a deer feels like, she thought.

The sirens wore down, as did the rain, but the red-and-white light bars continued to spin, casting eerie reflections against the buildings.

16

Four uniformed officers, guns drawn, used their car doors as shields and shouted, "Stop. Police. Do not move."

"Turn around. Put your hands in the air."

"Throw your weapon down."

"What weapon?" Mel called out, then realized the chrome light she held might appear to be a gun. "Okay, okay. It's only a flashlight." She threw it away from her body, and it broke, glass shattering as it struck the pavement.

"Back up slowly. Keep your hands where we can see them."

"It's me. Mel Walker. T-Bone's daughter."

A small crowd of loiterers and street walkers watched from a safe distance. They applauded the police and yelled, "Yeah. Caught a dangerous flashlight bandit, huh?" Laughter broke out among the bystanders, as they shared drinks from brown paper bags.

"Hi, Mel," one of the officers replied. He re-holstered his gun and motioned to the others to do the same. "We got a two-eleven call. Are you okay?"

"Yeah. But Johnnie, my associate, needs an ambulance. And there's a dead guy in the alley who needs the coroner."

❖ Chapter 3 ❖

The rain subsided to a fine misty spray. Yellow-and-black caution tape criss-crossed the street and alley for a hundred feet in either direction. Crime scene investigators snapped photos, identified and marked clues with numbered plastic signs, and scribbled data on forms on their clipboards. Several uniformed officers guarded the scene and managed the larger crowd that had gathered. The area, now bathed with portable light, illuminated an ambulance and a large, black van with white letters, "CORONER," across the rear doors.

A short distance away, Mel stood facing Detective Xavier "X-Ray" Ramirez, almost head-to-head, distracted by his dark piercing eyes, jet-black wavy hair, and well-toned body.

She shivered and rubbed her wet hands together, blowing into them.

X-Ray motioned to his unmarked police car. "You're drenched. Let's sit in the unit."

"I'm worried about Johnnie. I need to be with him."

"Let the EMT's do their job. He'll be on his way to the hospital in a minute. You can see him there. I'm sending one of my best men with Johnnie. Okay? Right now, this is a major crime scene and you're our only witness."

She knew that if it hadn't been for her dad, X-Ray would

never be one of Harbour Pointe's best known officers.

Detective William "T-Bone" Walker had commanded a stolen car sting operation, which led to the Tio gang's downfall. In those days X-Ray was a twelve-year-old lookout for the gang, but Walker caught him anyway. The kid not only had street smarts, but a keen sense of self-worth and a spark for genius. Walker recognized this and pulled X-Ray from the system, took him home to meet Mel and her mother, and made him attend school. X-Ray never left.

X-Ray earned the nickname from his ability to see through lies offered up as truths. He had heard it, used it himself, and managed to live through it.

"What were you and Johnnie doing here?" The question jerked Mel back to the present.

"We had an appointment."

"Who with?"

"A client."

"We're not going to play guessing games again, are we?" X-Ray opened the car door for Mel and got in beside her.

Mel's reply was a resounding, "I hope not."

"Are you packing?"

"My concealed weapons permit was pulled by Chief Murdoch. Did you forget?"

"Since you ignore the rules most of the time, I'll ask you again. Did you come here with a weapon tonight?"

"I love it when you get angry."

"Bullshit." X-Ray said, as Mel struggled to remove her wet raincoat.

Someone called out to X-Ray. He turned to talk with the officer, and Mel used the distraction to tuck her client's note inside one of the raincoat's inner pockets.

X-Ray told him, "You accompany the victim to the hospital and bring me that bullet. Don't break the chain of evidence, or I'll have your butt."

The officer nodded. X-Ray turned his attention back to Mel. "You almost got yourself killed here tonight. Don't tell me you and Johnnie came to a dark alley in the pouring rain to see a perfect stranger without one of you carrying a weapon. You couldn't be that dumb."

"I just got off the plane from Maui."

Another officer, carrying a pad and pencil, approached their car. X-Ray rolled down the car window again.

"The dead body's got no ID, sir."

"None at all?"

"No sir." The officer returned to the alley.

"And I didn't get an introduction before someone blew him away," Mel told X-Ray. She put the raincoat over the back of the seat in front of her, then crossed her arms, and placed both hands under her armpits for warmth.

"How did you know to meet him here?"

"I got a note in the mail."

X-Ray opened a palm and motioned with fingers, "Let's have it."

"What?"

"What do you think?"

Mel's head spun with questions that included how she would collect the balance of her ten thousand dollar fee. She said, "Sorry. I don't have it on me right now. If I can find it, I'll drop it by the department tomorrow. If that's okay with you?"

X-Ray gave her his famous, "Look me in the eyes and tell me the truth" stare.

Mel didn't flinch. She had played this game with him before.

20

They didn't call him X-Ray for nothing.

Another suited officer walked out of the alley and handed X-Ray a plastic bag. "We dug this out of the wall," he said.

"It's the bullet with your name on it, Mel," X-Ray said, as he examined it. "It's from a 9mm. Know anybody who owns a 9mm?"

Mel made a sweeping gesture across the entire scene and replied, "Hundreds."

X-Ray questioned Mel for another hour, long after the crowd dispersed and the ambulance had transported Johnnie to the hospital. X-Ray then called Harbour View on his cell phone.

"Surgical, please," he waited. "This is Detective Ramirez with the Harbour Pointe P.D. I need to check on a GSW patient. Johnnie Blake. Uh, huh. How much longer, you think? Is my officer still there? Fine, thank you."

X-Ray hung up and turned to Mel. "Johnnie's still in surgery. Should be in recovery by the time we get to the hospital."

"Gun Shot Wound . . . what a horrible mnemonic. I remember that's what you wrote on Dad's police report. I hated it then and I hate it now." Mel's cheeks tingled, raw from the rain and her contact with the asphalt.

"Want a ride?"

"No, thanks. I have the keys to the Pumpkin—you know, Johnnie's car. No point getting ticketed for parking here overnight. You know, if he's still in surgery, Johnnie's going to have a long night. Why don't you question him in the morning?" She put her raincoat back on as she squeezed the pocket containing her client's note.

21

X-Ray walked her to the Mustang. He hugged her, and kissed her on the forehead. "Okay. Tell Johnnie I'll be by early in the morning. For now, tell him to rest, and that's an order."

"I'll tell him."

X-Ray turned to go, then paused, "Oh, in all this mess, I forgot. Welcome back." He pointed his imaginary weapon at her with his index finger and winked.

Mel smiled, "Thanks, I missed you too."

She turned on the ignition. The Pumpkin's glass pipes made a "blubble, blubble," muffler sound in the night. The curious assortment of onlookers, who had brought traffic in the street to a virtual standstill, had paired up and vanished. Before she reached the next block, the heater and defogger, blowing full blast, cleared dew from the windshield.

As she sped to the hospital, three questions topped a long list. Who is our murdered client? Why was he killed? Why did the murderer shoot at Johnnie and me?

❖ Chapter 4 ❖

Harbour View Hospital was a five-story, white stucco, wide-windowed complex. It stood like a sentinel in the damp night, sterile and filled with memories of ghosts past.

Mel drove to the side entrance, slowed, and looked for a parking space. Dots of coastal humidity, like fireflies, danced below the hazy-yellow, overhanging lamps. An ambulance, with both doors open, had backed into the loading entrance and parked before two large steel doors. The hospital's medical team rushed the EMT's and gurney inside the building. The doors made a noise behind them that seemed to suck life from the air.

Mel sat in the car for a moment, listening to the tick of the cooling engine, and shivered. Doc Townsend would be waiting for her. He had tried every medical procedure he knew to save her son, Willie, struck by a hit-and-run driver, and later, her mother Carolyn, who died of breast cancer.

Inside, an elderly lady in a pink uniform sat talking on the telephone. Mel avoided eye contact and walked with authority past the front desk toward the surgical floor.

"Hi, Janeen." Mel tapped the ICU desktop.

A nurse looked up from her station, smiled, and mouthed, "I'll be right with you." After a few moments of conversation she hung up the phone. "Good evening, Mel. Wondered where you were." Mel followed her through two swinging doors that read, "Do Not Enter—ICU."

"X-Ray detained me at the crime scene a little longer than I thought. How's Johnnie?"

"He's resting. A little cranky, but otherwise okay."

"That's our Johnnie. He'll be fine." Mel lowered her voice. "He will be, won't he?"

"Sure," the nurse replied, smiling. "Bed two." Janeen motioned to a corner cubicle.

Mel pulled the curtain back. "Hi, big guy. How're you doing?" She brushed his hair back, leaned over, and kissed him on the forehead. He felt clammy and feverish.

"Lousy. It hurts like hell. But, great . . . great drugs." Johnnie managed a small smile through his pencil-thin lips and turned his head toward the IV drip.

"Has Doc been in since your surgery?"

"I had surgery?"

"Yeah. A bullet. You remember? You were shot."

"Oh, shit. I . . . was?"

"Yes."

"Did you shoot me?"

"No. Of course not. And I don't know who did. But we'll find out and get that bastard. You're in no condition to talk, so I better make this short. Don't tell X-Ray we have a note, you know, from our client? I want to keep that close to the vest for now."

"What vest? Did the guy have on a vest?"

"Never mind. You get some sleep."

"Where's the Pumpkin?" Johnnie's speech slurred on the "kin" part of the word.

"Don't worry. I'm driving it." Mel gently rubbed his arm.

24

"The meter-maids ticket-and-tow . . ."

"It won't be."

"Feed Scat for me." Johnnie closed his eyes and began to snore.

Mel shook his sleeping body. "Who's Scat?"

"Ticket-and-tow? Hmm. A good place to start." Mel drove the Pumpkin back toward *La Casa.* "Our client would have driven here. No mass transportation anywhere near this part of town," she thought.

The area seemed darker, and the shadows deeper than she remembered. Mel slowed, examining both sides of the street: cleaners, a beauty salon, an antique shop, real estate, and the restaurant. Their neon signs were off.

Mel parked the Mustang by the curb. She checked her watch against the closing times for each business. *La Casa* had been the last, at nine o'clock. It was now after midnight. So, any cars parked since the time of the shooting would have cold engines.

Using a small penlight, she walked a block through the dark neighborhood. The dank smells of sweat, urine, and unclaimed garbage assailed her. Returning to the Pumpkin, she walked an extra block, defining a broader circle. After turning the first corner near an industrial area, she spotted an older model, blue Chevrolet. She reached out and touched the hood. Cold. "That's a good sign. Let's see what else we have," she thought. She wrote down a description of the car, complete with license plate number.

It took ten minutes for Mel to reach the Pumpkin, having

seen no other vehicles in the area that matched her criteria. She started the engine and drove back to the parked Chevrolet. Mel left the fog lights on, approached the vehicle on foot, and tried the door. Not locked. Like a guy who might be in a hurry to leave?

She pushed her hair up and under a blue baseball hat she found in the Mustang's back seat. No use adding to the DNA in that car. She pulled out a tissue and opened the Chevrolet's door. No interior light came on. Another hint he may not want to be spotted. She leaned in and jiggled the overhead light. It came on when tightened.

"This must be the car," she thought.

Mel ran her fingers under the front seat, and after a moment searching, discovered a large set of keys from under the floor mat behind the seat rails. One key started the car. She turned off the ignition. The engine continued to run huffing and puffing before stopping, it seemed from exertion.

Now to relocate some evidence. "X-Ray is not going to be happy," she thought. "But I'm not exactly stealing it. Getting it off the street, so it won't get ticketed. Doing a public service by opening up a parking space for tomorrow. Sending it home safe and sound where the heirs can find it."

Mel continued to seduce herself into believing she was not obstructing justice, while rummaging through the glove compartment. There she found the registration papers.

"Well, hello Mr. Paul Cooper of Santa Ana, California. Where's the rest of my retainer?"

❖ Chapter 5 ❖

Mel called directory assistance. One Paul Cooper answered the phone with a yawn, suggesting he had been asleep. He told Mel his Lexus was parked in his garage and slammed the phone down. At the home of the other Paul Cooper, she got an answering machine with a sour, "You know what to do. I do too. So start, already." Then a cough followed by a beep.

"Has to be my man," she thought.

Now, to get both the Pumpkin and the Chevrolet off the streets without being noticed, or making someone she liked an accessory to obstruction of justice or worse. "I can't call a tow truck or a taxi. Both will have records of the trip." It was a tough call.

Harbour Pointe is a sleepy beach community hugged by the winding four-lane Pacific Coast Highway. Fishermen, surfers, and longtime, family-owned businesses line the ocean on the west side of PCH. Fast-food franchises line the streets on the east side of the highway. Many west side bumper stickers read, "Working is for those who can't surf." East side stickers read, "Vote Republican."

Mel tapped her foot, and looked up and down the street. She thought, "Okay, I drive Paul Cooper's car to T.J.'s on the Back Bay. Patrol cop will stop me for sure if I walk back. Maybe

Bernie's. It's near. And they have a parking lot. Won't that be funny? Stashing my client's car at a cop's hangout."

She drove the Chevrolet to the graveled lot behind Bernie's, locked the car, kept the keys, and walked back to the Pumpkin.

Exhausted from her long walk, she slept in one spot all night, or so it seemed when the first rays of sun hit her eyes. Her head throbbed with pain. She rolled over and squinted at the digital numbers on the clock.

Jeez. Seven o'clock.

After she showered and washed her hair, Rosa, her housekeeper, knocked on the bathroom door and said, "Welcome home. Want some breakfast?"

"Aloha, Rosa. Just a bite. I've got to go to the police department and the hospital this morning. Ah!"

Rosa jerked the bathroom door open and rushed in. "What's the matter? Did you cut yourself?"

"Oh, my God. Look." Mel wiped the foggy mirror and leaned closer. She held a wide-toothed comb in one hand and one strand of her hair in the other.

Rosa laughed, "Don't be a baby. It's just a gray hair."

"No." Mel moaned, "It's much more than that."

"So," Rosa put one hand on her hip, "you got one gray hair. Hmm." She turned, walked out of the room, pulled the sheets and bedspread neatly under the pillows, then called over her shoulder, "Welcome to middle age, Mel. Join the crowd."

Mel squared her shoulders and announced, "Well, I'm going to be different. Don't your people get gray hair?"

"We, El Salvadorian. Jet black hair . . . like all our Mayan family."

Rosa's strong ancestral features: blunt, coarse, ebony hair, short, stocky body, and small, round face supported deep cocoa eyes and a warm smile.

"Well, I don't want to get gray hair."

"It's better than the alternative. You can think about old age during breakfast. I'll get you some prunes."

"I don't have time."

"You just got home. Are you already in trouble?" Rosa asked.

"Yeah."

Mel took her cuticle scissors, and cut off the gray strand, pressed a pimple on her chin between her fingers until it became rosy, then hummed a death march. Terrific. Old age and puberty on the same day.

Rosa's mother Analynn, and her family were El Salvadorian. Born in California, Rosa became the housekeeper when Analynn retired.

Mel's attorney ex-husband had helped Rosa and her family incorporate their domestic services business, and it provided income and jobs for everyone. The business had flourished, and Rosa could manage it and do well financially without working herself. But she wouldn't leave Mel.

After Mel's mother and father died, Mel suspected Rosa had assumed the responsibility of parenting, since Rosa continued to show up several days a week to cook, clean, and give advice.

She pulled on jeans, a white, cotton shirt and tennis shoes, looked at herself critically in the mirror, and thought, "Wonder if there are any more gray hairs lurking about?" She added a blue baseball cap over damp hair and bounced downstairs.

Smells of salsa and strains of a cha-cha-cha filled the kitchen.

29

"Why is the Pumpkin in the driveway?" Rosa asked, stirring eggs.

"I drove it home last night. Johnnie's in the hospital."

Rosa spun around and clasped her hands in prayer, "*Madre Mia!* What happened?"

"He got shot. It's a long story. He's gonna be fine," Mel assured her.

"Did you shoot him?" She brandished a spatula.

"Of course not."

Rosa wiped her hands on her apron. "I will go with you to the hospital. Johnnie will need me."

Mel appreciated Rosa's motherly plea and hugged her. The smell of fresh vanilla exuded from Rosa's clothes. "No reason for you to go. Besides, I need to see X-Ray first. We should have Johnnie home later today. I don't want him to stay at the apartment alone. You could ready the downstairs bedroom for him. Make some of his favorite dishes and we can coddle him here. I promise I'll call you later with a full medical report."

Rosa returned to the stove, her hands moving quickly and steadily. She opened and slammed doors and drawers, then turned and handed Mel a brown bag and a cup of coffee. "Then," Rosa said, in a shooing manner, "you must go right now and call me very soon."

"Do we have some plastic wrap? I need a long sheet of it. To go."

Rosa made a face, then went to the pantry and returned with a box. She tore off a long piece, which promptly stuck to itself as it hung in the air. She handed it to Mel.

Outside, Mel opened the trunk and carefully wrapped her client's note and the envelope separately in the plastic, then placed the bundle in the trunk of her own car under a cloth heatshield. She turned on the Mustang's ignition, and, as she backed out of the driveway, saw Rosa sweeping the front stoop. Mel rolled the car window down and shouted, "By the way, Rosa, do you know a Scat?"

Rosa smiled, nodded, and closed the lacquered front doors behind her.

❖ Chapter 6 ❖

Fifty officers work for the Harbour Pointe Police Department. They serve and protect forty-one thousand, full and part-time citizens and cover seven square miles of Southern California's prime coastal real estate. Chief Murdoch, a tough, cranky, career cop, supervises three captains, six divisions and twelve bureaus, as well as a full complement of contract civil service employees and a state-of-the-art computer communications operation.

The one story, whitewashed, stucco police building resembled a long and narrow, windowless tomb. A huge satellite dish with several antennas blanketed the flat roof. Mel parked and entered the building, acknowledging the civil service employee at the front desk who buzzed her into the squad room. Phones rang. Men and women chattered in small groups. Half-a-dozen officers were story-boarding a case outlined on a large blackboard, shouting out ideas. Smells of fresh coffee and donuts filled the air. Chief Murdoch spotted Mel and lumbered over, giving her a deep bear hug.

"Aloha. Isn't that what they say in Hawaii?" he asked.

"That's right. Aloha." She returned the hug.

Chief Murdoch and Mel's dad had gone to the police academy together and later forged a thirty-year partnership. When the time came for promotions, T-Bone Walker wanted to stay a detective, while his friend, Murdoch, rose through the ranks.

Murdoch's thinning salt-and-pepper hair appeared wild and out of control. So did the bushy eyebrows which he now twisted and hand-combed as they talked. "Just like your old man. Not home two hours, and we have a one-eighty-seven, and a GSW. How is Johnnie this morning?"

"I don't know. X-Ray told me to come by here first, so we could go over some things. We'll drive over to see Johnnie later. When I saw him last night, he was very groggy."

"Yeah. Been shot myself. Burns like shit." He rubbed his right elbow. "And it's the gift that keeps on giving. I can tell the change in temperature with this elbow."

"I remember," Mel replied. "Where's X-Ray?"

X-Ray pushed through a door from the evidence room and entered, carrying some papers and talking with an employee Mel did not recognize. X-Ray said, "Good morning. 'Bout time you got here." He turned to the woman beside him and added, "I want to introduce you to our new evidence clerk, Audrey Lewis. We call her Lou. This is Camellia Walker. We call her Mel."

The two women shook hands and smiled. Lou was several inches taller than Mel and X-Ray, and enviously thin. Long arms and lankier legs, a chocolate-brown body and a model's face, with high cheekbones and perfectly arched eyebrows made her a stunning woman.

Mel shook her head. "You are gorgeous. I don't think I'm going to like you."

"It's all in the genes," Lou explained.

"She ate two donuts before her first cup of coffee," X-Ray volunteered.

"Oh, now I know you and I can never be friends," Mel laughed.

33

X-Ray said, "Will you excuse us, Lou? Mel was involved in a homicide last night and brought me some evidence that we'll check in with you later. You did, didn't you, Mel?"

"Not exactly."

"Do you have the note or not?"

"I'm sure it must be somewhere. I've checked the house, the car, and the office. I just can't find it. That's why I was late." Mel did not look X-Ray in the eye as she spoke.

X-Ray raised an eyebrow and took Mel by the arm. Lou backed away from the confrontation and returned to the evidence room. "Don't play games, Mel. You're too meticulous. I know it's in your files, somewhere."

"I promise. I'll find the client's note and bring it in." At the right time, she thought.

X-Ray sighed, "Ready to go see Johnnie?"

"Yeah. Can I drive the Pumpkin over and meet you there? I have other appointments today."

"Sure. I'll bet Rosa is putting her nursing hat on as we speak."

"That's what she said when I left home."

"I need to make one stop before going to the hospital. I'll join you there."

"One stop? Where?"

"It dawned on me this morning that whoever got murdered had to drive there. I ordered the Crime Scene Unit out this morning to look for a vehicle. I want to see how they're doing."

❖ Chapter 7 ❖

Mel opened the door and peeked around the corner to find Johnnie sitting up in bed and picking at his breakfast.

"Ah," Mel said, looking at his food tray. "It's Wednesday. Must be bile broth and green Jell-O day."

"Hi," Johnnie said. His voice faint.

"Aren't you pathetic? Wanting a little sympathy today?"

"Wanting some of Rosa's *huevos rancheros* today."

"I can't blame you. That looks, well, watery."

"It is." Johnnie plopped his spoon into the pale yellow liquid and splashed some onto his bed covers.

Mel laughed. "Now, you've made a mess." She began to wipe the spill.

"It isn't going to hurt you to clean up after me for once. I'm the one who got shot." Johnnie held his left hand to his bandaged right arm and shoulder. "I'm worrying how I'm going to do everyday things. I'm right-handed, you know."

"Rosa has all that worked out. When Doc Townsend and the surgeon release you, you're coming home with me."

"Oh, brother." Johnnie scrunched down in the bed.

"No, dear. That's 'oh, Mother.' That's what she plans for you."

"Ugh. When can I go home?"

35

"I'll leave a call for the doctors, if they don't come in while I'm here. Listen. I need to talk with you before X-Ray gets here. We need our stories to match."

"Oh oh, that sounds like conspiracy."

"No. Not really." Mel said, adding, "Just an information slowdown."

"Sure," Johnnie nodded.

"First, I told X-Ray that I couldn't find our client's note."

"Just tell X-Ray that you gave it to me. Anyway why are you hiding it?"

"I want to find out more about our client. Also, I'd have to fake evidence by attaching some kind of bill to it. Remember? It said something like, 'If you want the rest of this,' yada, yada, yada. And I'm not ready to give up the ten thousand dollars yet."

"You'll need it to post bail when he catches you," Johnnie said, as he chuckled. "And what's number two?"

"Okay. Second, I figured out that our client must have driven there. Therefore, his car would be parked nearby. So, after I left here last night, I went back to the scene and found it."

"And?"

"I moved our client's vehicle."

"Oh shit. Where?"

"I think the less you know, the better off you'll be."

"You mean when they indict you for tampering with two pieces of evidence in an ongoing murder investigation?" Johnnie gave her a look.

"No. X-Ray wouldn't do that . . . exactly."

"Don't kid yourself. Chief Murdoch pulled your concealed weapon permit, didn't he?"

"Oh, that. All I did was shoot some bad guys. I didn't kill anybody." Mel straightened the sheets and bedcover.

"Why did you move the car?" Johnnie asked.

"I know who our client is . . . or rather . . . was. I found his registration in the glove compartment. He's Paul Cooper. I have his keys and his address. I'd like to look at his house and try to find out why he wanted our help. Also, I have half a ten thousand dollar bond too. Remember?"

"Right . . . assuming that was his car. It could belong to someone who may have gotten lucky at the bar and rode home with another person."

"Oh, hell, I didn't think about that." Mel paced the small room.

"So, assuming that was his car, what next?" Johnnie asked.

"Well, he is . . . or was . . . our client, and I have a fiduciary responsibility to help him."

"Oh, Christ," Johnnie said. "I see where this is headed. You're adding breaking and entering to the charge. Thank you, Lord, for keeping me in the hospital while all this is happening. I wouldn't want to be in your shoes when X-Ray finds out. Where is he, by the way?"

"This morning X-Ray thought about the victim's car. He and the Crime Scene Unit are out looking for the vehicle."

Johnnie pulled the sheets over his head, and Mel heard a muffled, "I know nothing. I see nothing. I hear nothing."

She leaned over and kissed the top of the sheet. "Love you, Johnnie. I've got to run. Will check in later."

"Be careful, honey," Johnnie called out, as she dashed from the room.

❖ Chapter 8 ❖

Mel and Johnnie, with help from Rosa's family, had transformed T-Bone and Carole's home into the offices of Walker Investigations. Mel knew her mom and dad would love the idea of having her there, working and sharing ideas with others.

Long, thin, gray clouds scattered over the skies like grainy pull-taffy as seagulls, buffeted by offshore winds, circled the beach community. The smell of freshly mowed grass, ozone, and not so fresh fish, preceded Mel into the subdivision.

The small, one-story frame house had a newly painted, white exterior, a manicured lawn, a few eucalyptus trees, and neatly trimmed roses her mother had nurtured so lovingly.

Mel smiled and pulled into the driveway. Johnnie had once lived with Mel. But after they converted the house, he coveted space of his own, and now lived in a large garage apartment in back.

She parked the Pumpkin in the garage, locked it behind her and entered the house through the back door.

She kicked her shoes off, pulled a cold drink from the refrigerator, and headed for her office. Johnnie had converted one bedroom into his office; the master bedroom was hers. The other bedroom served as their conference room and was stacked high with law books. The low-pile carpeting felt plush under her feet. She turned on the computer and flipped through her mail while the equipment warmed up.

Mel checked the name Paul Cooper through voter's registration, which verified the address on his vehicle ownership records. She got an age from that record—56. Mel then ran his name through several criminal checks in both Orange and Los Angeles Counties.

No record. That's a good sign, she thought.

Mel pulled up his birth certificate on the screen, found his social security number and birth date. She hit the PRINT button when something caught her attention. The letters DECEASED stared out at her in bold black letters. A death certificate check revealed Paul Cooper had died in the late 1950s. Mel signed on the Internet and scanned the *Los Angeles Times* beginning in 1957. She checked each page. The ads made her chuckle. Gas was thirty-two cents a gallon. Consumers complained about the rising costs of maintaining their brand new sixteen-hundred dollar Volkswagens. The obits for June 1959 jumped out at her. Paul Cooper was killed in a car accident on his prom night . . . on the eve of his seventeenth birthday.

Why was my client using a dead man's ID? Who are you really, she thought. And why are you hiding behind an alias?

Half an hour later, Mel retrieved her gunmetal gray SL Mercedes and drove to the Santa Ana address on Paul Cooper's registration. She spotted the wood-frame house, drove casually past it, parked on the next street, and walked back. She pulled her hat down closer to her eyebrows, put on her gloves, and walked with purpose toward the front door stepping over two days of newspapers. She knocked. No one responded. Mel used the end of one key to lift the mailbox top. Mail, dated several days earlier, lay inside the box. She pulled each envelope forward. None were addressed to a Mrs. Paul Cooper. Using the key, she opened the door and stepped across the threshold.

"Jeez."

Green-patterned sofa pillows were strewn about the room. The matching couch and two chairs were upended and papers cluttered the living and dining room floors. She ran her fingers under drawers in the kitchen and a breakfront in the dining room. Nothing taped here. Mel opened a desk drawer and found a small, red-vinyl telephone book. A paper clip on the back page held a driver's license, a social security card, and a credit card in the name of David Erickson. The license photo was that of her client. She copied the information from Erickson's papers on the back of one of her checks.

Who the hell are you? David Erickson maybe?

Several medical invoices from a Dr. Sarah Reynolds and the Newport Surgical Center were stacked neatly at the bottom of several other bills.

Mel looked behind every picture in the house. Nothing taped there and no hidden safes on the walls.

She entered the master bedroom. The walls had been sponge-painted a light tan. The king-sized mattress lay crossways on a brass railing. She lifted it and found nothing between the mattress and the bedframe. A tan and black-striped bedspread and two shams lay crumpled on the floor. She entered a large walk-in closet. Plain, unremarkable casual shirts and cotton slacks hung neatly, by color, on a single pole. But no blue-jeans. And no tossing here. What they were looking for is larger than a bread box and cannot be hidden in clothes.

Two well-worn brown suits with empty pockets dangled at the far end of the closet. Beside those suits, five identical white dress shirts hung in a neat row. On a black plastic hanger were five striped ties in varying shades of brown. Two pairs of brown wing-tipped shoes; one with tassels, one without, lay side-by-side on the floor.

What you want to bet he was an accountant? Too neat, too brown. Almost old-fashioned. Nothing feminine here. Single, a loner, no family. No friends. A mad bomber? No personal pictures or knickknacks.

Mel picked up the telephone receiver and hit the automatic redial.

"Hello," a pleasant female voice said. "Connelly residence."

"Connelly?" Mel replied. "Thank you. Is this the family of ... excuse me I can't read this? Is it Paul? Maybe David?"

"I have a son named Peter." The voice sounded like an elderly woman.

"Peter. Yes. I see that now. Is that Connelly with an 'elly' or 'ally'?"

"C-o-n-n-e-l-l-y."

"Is Peter in, please?" Mel asked.

"No. He doesn't live here. But, I can have him call you, if you'd like to leave a number. He's my only son and I should hear from him sometime today."

"Thanks. I believe I have his number. Is it . . .?" And Mel repeated the number on the telephone she was using.

"Yes. Well, you have it then. Have a nice day." The motherly voice faded into a click.

"Better than you will, lady," Mel said to the dial tone.

Mel dialed the number for time service, listened to the

41

operator, then hung up. If the police or the murderer thought to check the last number called, they won't bother that little lady. At least for the time being.

She opened the refrigerator door. On the top shelf, she spotted one-half an orange sealed in a plastic container, three soft apples, lunch meat, and a bottle of mustard. The next shelf held a partially full bottle of nonfat milk. In the freezer section, she moved around several, ice-glazed, mystery items. On the bottom of one, Mel felt something sticking to the ice. A key in a plastic bag. She turned the faucet on, soaked the key off the packet, and pocketed it.

Mel walked back to her car without encountering anyone. She took off her gloves and turned on the ignition. She allowed several cars to pass before pulling away from the curb. A black sedan with tinted windows fell into traffic behind her. She picked up her cell phone and called Dr. Reynolds' office for an appointment.

❖ Chapter 9 ❖

Dr. Reynolds' fashionable southwestern-style office was tucked away on a side street near Newport Beach's elegant shopping mecca, appropriately named *Fashion Island*. Mel parked on the street and walked to the office. She passed two young valets dressed in white shirts, black shorts, and black bow ties.

Tall brick walls surrounded the physician's office. Mel pushed the buzzer.

"Yes?" a feminine voice called out. "How may we help you?"

"Mel Walker to see Dr. Reynolds. I have an appointment."

A sharp buzz sounded. Mel pushed the carved wooden door and entered an atrium. Large tropical ginger flowers, fragrant plumeria, and colorful pansies filled every corner of the compound. She walked across large, terra cotta pavers that wove in and around immense planters filled with queen palms and split-leaf philodendrons. A woman with a bright smile and gleaming white teeth greeted her from behind an etched-glass reception counter. Her face was like porcelain: white and flawless.

"Miss Walker?"

"Yes," Mel replied, and held one finger over her cheek. Why did I pick that blackhead this morning? It's probably red as a beacon, she thought.

"Dr. Reynolds is just coming out of surgery. Please have a seat. She should be with you in a few moments." The voice was as perfect as the face.

Mel selected a red and brown, silk-covered chair and sat. She picked up a *Glamour* magazine and pushed her sunglasses on her forehead. A few moments passed when a white-uniformed attendant entered the room. "Miss Walker?"

"Yes."

"Dr. Reynolds will see you now." She held the door open, and Mel followed the nurse down a long wide hallway to a corner office.

A striking redhead in white knit pants and a three-quarter length white smock stood to greet Mel. She wore a simple, almost masculine, gold chain necklace and no other jewelry.

Mel extended her right hand. "My father always said you can judge a person by a handshake."

"How'd I do?" Dr. Reynolds asked, motioning Mel to a chair near the desk.

"Good. Nice, firm but strong. Must be all that skin tugging and sucking, huh?"

Dr. Reynolds laughed. "Well, I never heard it expressed quite that way. But I guess so. How can I help you? I've got a patient in pre-op and two in post-op. You said this was urgent."

"Thank you for seeing me today. You do your surgery at this location?"

"Most of it. We have two surgical suites and a large post-op recovery room."

"Makes for privacy?"

"That's an important consideration for performing plastic surgery . . . privacy for our patients."

"You have an anesthesiologist on staff?"

"Actually, I have one I use most often, but he's an independent contractor."

"Kinda like 'have gas, will travel'?"

Dr. Reynolds laughed again, "Yes, I guess so." She tapped a pencil against the desktop. "I'm busy, Miss Walker. Is this about some insurance matter? I have an office manager who . . ."

"No. No, actually I'm here about one of your clients. Paul Cooper."

"And what's your connection to Mr. Cooper?" the doctor asked.

"I'm an investigator. He hired me to do some work. I'd like to know more about him, before I decide whether or not to take his case."

"And he told you I am his doctor?" Dr. Reynolds asked. She nodded as she spoke.

"Yes." One more lie today isn't going to hurt.

"Well, as an investigator, I'm sure you understand the doctor-patient relationship. The only thing I can really discuss, without a signed authorization, of course . . . do you have one, by the way?"

"No. I don't. Actually, being hired as an investigator is a rather loose process. I did get a note from him, asking for my help, no real . . . you know . . . official contract."

"Do you have the note with you? Maybe it could be construed as an authorization." Dr. Reynolds leaned over the edge of the desk and placed one hand forward, palm up.

"Yes, I understand. But I've misplaced the note. However, I assure you, I am working for him."

"Well then, Miss Walker, I could only verify he is a patient of mine. Beyond that, I really can't elaborate."

"Can we talk hypothetically for a moment?"

"Certainly."

"Tell me some reasons men get facelifts? I may have a friend interested . . ."

"Vanity is as important to men as it is to women."

"Really?" Wait until I tell Johnnie.

"I have some written materials that may explain." Dr. Reynolds reached into a side drawer, withdrew a brochure and several pieces of papers.

Mel took them. "So," she opened the brochure, "men and women are vain. That, I understand. But, why would a middle-age man living very modestly, seemingly unemployed, and not married, want to have reconstructive work?"

Dr. Reynolds leaned on her desk with both elbows, her right hand to her smooth flawless cheek, and whispered, "He may be expecting a new relationship, want to remove an old scar, like from a burn or accident, or laser off a tattoo . . ."

"Or hide from someone or something?" Mel interrupted.

"Yes." Dr. Reynolds drew out the "s" response.

"Do you operate on fingerprints?"

"Can I or do I?"

"Both."

"I can, yes. It's called sanding and it's done on people with burns and other scars. It's very painful and the healing time is very long. Do I? Not really. That's not a procedure I'm often called upon to perform."

"Is it successful?"

"Fingerprints cannot be changed one hundred percent. The body has a way of remembering. It's not permanent."

"Do some patients make installment payments?"

"And cash is nice too." Dr. Reynolds smiled.

"Does insurance cover any procedure?"

"Several, yes. Breast reconstruction after mastectomies, some birth defects, rhinoplasty, you know," she pointed at her nose, "deviated septum, scar reduction, burns."

A beeper rang. Each woman looked down at her own waistband.

"It's mine, Miss Walker. Post-op review." She stood. "Is there anything else I can help you with?"

"What would be the recovery period for someone, like Mr. Cooper, before he could be seen in public?"

"A full facelift, rhinoplasty, face and forehead lift, blepharoplasty . . . the eyelids, and maybe an implant or two would take almost five hours. The patient would then require twenty-four to forty-eight hours of monitoring for blood clots and irregular heart beats. And he or she could be presentable in about two weeks with some mild swelling and bruising."

"Ouch. That sounds painful."

"Ah, but the rewards . . ." Dr. Reynolds raised a hand to the ceiling.

"The state requires you to keep records?"

"Seven to ten years, depending on the patient's procedures."

"Is there ever any time you would share Mr. Cooper's medical treatment with me?"

"Only with a signed medical authorization. Now if you will excuse me, I have a patient waiting. However, if you should ever need my services, I hope you'll call me."

"It's never too early?"

"Or too late. The consultation is absolutely free."

Dr. Reynolds opened a door behind her desk and disappeared into a back room, leaving Mel alone. She walked toward the exit sign and passed a file room.

No one here. Assuming those records might still be here,

47

wonder how long it would take me to find the COOPER, PAUL file? She took one step over the threshold.

"The exit is this way, Miss Walker." A nurse appeared behind Mel, took her by the arm, and guided her toward the exit.

❖ Chapter 10 ❖

On the road again, Mel placed a call to the Orange County Coroner's office.

"Hi, Sally. It's Mel. Is Barry in?"

"Aloha. How was your vacation?"

"Not long enough."

"Hold and I'll see if I can find him." Music took the place of Sally's voice. Mel's mind wandered. Barry Zabel, happily married with six children, had been a friend as long as Mel could remember. A shock of white hair streaked from the top of his head to his forehead; the rest of his hair remained astonishingly black.

"And I'll pull any more suckers I find," she said out loud, unaware Barry had picked up the phone.

"Pull what? That sounds painful." Barry laughed.

"A gray hair I found in my head today."

"Only one?"

"For a woman, that's all it takes."

He chuckled again. "Guess you're right. Welcome back from Maui. Tan and lovely?"

"No, pale and lonely."

"Too bad I'm taken, Mel."

She sighed, "Sure is."

"What's on your mind?"

"Want lunch?" Mel asked.

"Okay. Bernie's? In . . . ah . . . about," Mel could hear paper shuffling. "Half an hour?"

"Can you hold? I have another call. Hello, Mel speaking."

"Hi. Hungry?"

"Hi, X-Ray. Yeah. I could eat a bite. I have Barry on the other line. Want to join us?"

"Bernie's?"

"Yeah. See ya."

"Say, Barry. That was X-Ray. He'll join us. I'm calling about a John Doe. Did you get a Doe today?"

"Several. Why? Interested in taking my forensics class again?"

"Yuck. No. However, one John Doe is . . . or rather was . . . a client of mine."

"And his name is?"

"Uh," big lie coming up, "I don't know yet. I'm still working on developing that."

"Let me know when you ID him. We need to notify next of kin. I like to move them out quickly. Give the family some closure, you know."

"Sure. You got it. Okay, meet you at Bernie's."

Nothing like a little guilt trip from Barry to get my day going, Mel thought.

Surfers, looking for that special parallel parking spot against the curb, slowed traffic on Pacific Coast Highway. The congestion created enough stop-and-go traffic for Mel to reflect on how careful she would have to be, not to give away her client's name before X-Ray identified him.

Bernie's Café was housed in a small, wooden building on a graveled corner lot on Pacific Coast Highway. This had been her father's favorite haunt. A warm and charming redhead named Cookie, and her gruff, cigar chewing husband, Bernie, dished '50s music, plate-overflowing chicken-fried steaks smothered in cream gravy, and root beer floats to all the local cops and highway patrolmen. Cookie and Bernie were "friendlies," folks who didn't repeat stories they overheard.

Mel parked and scanned the area. She did not see her client's blue Chevrolet. The back screen door announced her arrival with a screech. She waved at the bald-headed Bernie, who stood behind the half-wall in the kitchen, a cigar in one hand, and a plate of food in the other.

"Hi, Bernie."

"What's happening?" he asked.

"Not much. How's business?"

"Can't complain."

"Who'd listen?" Cookie interrupted as she cleaned a Formica table and swiped the red vinyl booth with a towel.

"Hi, Cookie. I'm waiting for X-Ray and Barry."

"Take this one, Mel. I'll get you some setups. What'll you drink? Diet something?"

"Anything. Yeah."

Taut and wrinkle free, Cookie smelled of gardenias and wore a fresh clean white apron around the tiniest waist Mel had ever seen on a woman approaching fifty. Mel placed both hands on her own hips.

Like I could touch left fingers to right fingers with *this* body, she thought enviously, as she sat.

51

Cookie moved in time with a Little Richard song and patted one of the carrot red curls in her '50s hairstyle.

Mel smiled, then had a twinge of guilt. *What if Johnnie is right and I stole the wrong car?*

Cookie delivered silverware and two coffees and a cola. Before she had time to speak, the back door squeaked once more and X-Ray and Barry joined her.

"Hi, guys," Cookie said. "Coffee's fresh and hot."

"Thanks," X-Ray replied.

"I'll take a tuna-fish sandwich on wheat, toasted, with that coffee," Barry said.

X-Ray twirled his fingers in a circle, "Double that order. How 'bout you, Mel?"

"Okay. That's simple. Make it three," she replied.

Each man entered the booth from opposite sides placing Mel between them. Barry had a large white envelope that he passed to X-Ray.

"Here are the prints on our Doe. That should tell us who he is." Barry said.

"So what do you know about him other than that he'd had plastic surgery?" Mel asked.

"How'd you know that?" X-Ray asked.

"Sure . . . I . . . ah . . . saw his face at the scene, remember?"

"Oh, yeah. Right. Well. He paid a lot of money for this surgery, I can tell you that," Barry said.

"What do you mean?" X-Ray said.

"A full facelift, eyebrows, chin and cheek implants, nose, bags removed, ears pinned back. Full make-over, including hair plugs . . . brown ones."

"You mean I could have new hair put in my skull? In the color of my choice?" Mel asked.

"Sure. Say, you aren't still worried about your gray hair?" Barry laughed.

"What gray hair?" X-Ray leaned over and picked at her curls.

Mel pushed him away. "Cut that out. As a matter of fact, that's exactly what I did."

"What?" both men asked.

"Cut it out. I had one gray hair this morning. I took that sucker off clear to the root."

"Mel, you know what they say?" Barry offered.

"What?"

"For every gray hair you lose, two more grow in its place." Barry and X-Ray laughed.

"Shit." Mel thumped both elbows on the table.

"Hair plugs sound painful," X-Ray said.

"Sure does. Anybody's work you recognize?" Mel asked.

"No. But top drawer. I'm checking on surgeons in the area now. I should know in a few days."

"Can you tell who did the work from the implants? Do they have lot numbers or any identifying marks like there are on the breast implants?" Mel asked.

"How would you know so much about that?" X-Ray leaned back and pointed his index finger at her.

"I saw it on TV."

Barry interrupted, "Mel's right. You can get numbers off breast implants. Unfortunately, there's no such thing on the chin and cheek work. But I've made some calls and we should know something in the next day or so."

"By then I'll have those prints run and we'll have him identified," X-Ray said.

"Well, if you find out who my client is before I do, you let me know. Okay?" Mel asked.

"Sure."

Cookie delivered lunch bringing extra napkins and ketchup. She refilled the coffee cups and left the trio to talk.

After lunch, Mel said, "Look guys, I have some catching up to do at the office, so . . ."

"Including looking for that note from your client. You know, the one you can't find?" X-Ray added.

"Right." Mel placed seven dollars under the salt-and-pepper shakers. X-Ray rose and gave her a brief hug. She gripped her handbag under her arm, said "Goodbye, everybody," and left.

In the parking lot, Mel noticed a dark, older model sedan with tinted windows, which had not been there when she arrived.

Only X-Ray and Barry came inside and no one left. Both of their cars were parked on either side of hers.

Mel pulled onto Pacific Coast Highway, headed toward her office and picked up the phone to call Johnnie. She glanced in the rear view mirror. The black sedan fell into traffic behind her.

So who are you? Mel thought. Where have I seen you before? Behind me when I left Cooper's home.

❖ Chapter 11 ❖

"You sound distracted," Johnnie said. "Is the cell phone breaking up?"

"No. I don't think so. But I think I'm being followed."

"Shit, Mel. Drive straight to the police department, and I'll call and tell them you're coming in."

"No. He or she is not being aggressive. Just laying back. Watching me. Wish they'd pull close. I'd like to get the license number."

"I can tell you what the plate says. It reads, 'I'm the asshole who shot your client and your best friend in the entire world'."

"No, it doesn't," she replied, and glanced again in the mirror. "How do you know?"

"That's too many letters."

"Smart-ass. Both doctors released me so I can go home. I'm here in the hospital with my trigger finger in a sling, but you have your gun, don't you?"

"Nope. It's in the safe at the office, and that's where I'm headed. I can't get in trouble for protecting my office if I have to use it, now can I?"

"Probably not. But you definitely could get killed. Mel, maybe you didn't get a good look at our client. He's dead. And me, almost. Do not go home. Come get me first. You'll be . . ."

Static interrupted and disconnected the line.

The tail continued to follow Mel, as she made several circuitous turns on the way to the office. She pulled into the driveway, took her purse and keys, and walked to the front door without glancing around. Once inside, she shut the door, ducked, and crawled toward the floor safe in the dining room. She pulled out her Beretta, checked the clip and the safety, then inched her way to the dining room window. As she pulled back the blind, the sedan slowly passed her house.

Mel counted to ten, tried to slow her heartbeat and walked to the front door. Once outside, she let her left arm hang down, partially hiding the weapon at the back of her thigh. She ran to the curb, glanced up and down the street, but didn't see the car nor any pedestrians.

She sprinted around the side of the house past her car and the garage. Mel lifted the hook on the gate lock and stepped quietly into the alley.

Empty.

"Hi, kitty," Mel whispered to a young cat whose long black-and-white fur bounced in the air.

Mel returned to the front of the house and, once inside, locked the door.

She poured a glass of water and snacked on a graham cracker on the way to her office; then she pulled the dining room blinds back and waited. The street remained still and empty. She closed the blinds and stepped into her office. She flipped on her computer and munched on the cracker while the machine warmed up.

On the second chew of the first bite, something brushed her leg. Mel snatched the Beretta off the desk, pushed the captain's chair back and stood, feet wide apart, both hands on the trigger.

"Purr," was the first sound she heard. The kitten she had seen in the alley brushed against the edge of the desk and the chair leg. "Purr."

"Oh, no. Don't tell me you're Scat?"

"Purr," the engine ran louder.

"Oh, where did we get you?" Mel laid the gun on the desk and leaned over to pet the intruder. "More importantly, how'd you get in this locked and secure house?"

The black-and-white ball ducked Mel's grasp, opting to stand on the other side of the desk out of reach.

"Okay. So, you don't want to be touched. But, I'll bet you want to be fed. Am I right?"

The cat turned, its tail high in the air, nose straight ahead, and walked toward the kitchen.

"I'll be right with you. I need to check something first."

Mel pulled up voter's registration files on Peter Connelly. His social security number appeared on the line next to his name. She then opened the National Crime Information Center Website and entered her access code, then Peter's information. The blue triangle turned and the hourglass suggested a search engine was processing her request.

"Okay," Mel said, as she entered the kitchen, "where did Johnnie put your food? I'll bet you're hungry."

The kitten leaped to the counter top and sat.

Mel opened the refrigerator and pulled out a can of cat food that had been covered with a plastic top. She scooped out the contents into one dish she found near the door and added fresh water to another. "So, you're the newest member of our family. Welcome home, Scat. Now, I'll tell you a secret, if you tell me yours. How did you get inside?"

The cat eagerly devoured the food and purred like a machine gun. Mel checked all the windows and doors again. "Huh. Got me fooled. You must have followed me through the front door. You are one fast dude." Mel squatted and patted Scat once. That was allowed.

Mel returned to the computer. Two words were highlighted on the screen. "Bank Robbery."

"Jesus. The Western Guaranty Bank in Los Angeles." She dropped into the chair. "Shit. That's FBI territory. What are my chances of getting information from them?" Mel wrote down the six-digit file number and Peter's date of birth. The file number was cross-referenced to two additional files. She copied those numbers down, then turned to the FBI's Website.

Below the gold seal, Mel read, "The Los Angeles Field Office of the FBI is the second largest field office of the 56 Field Offices in the United States. Los Angeles services 40,000 square miles, a population of over 15.5 million, and seven counties in the Central District of California."

Oh, yeah. They're going to be really happy to hear from me.

She decided to send an e-mail first, seeking advice under the Freedom of Information Act. Mel typed the file numbers and asked that someone who might help, please contact her. The telephone rang. "Walker Investigations. Mel Walker speaking."

"You're not dead yet."

"Nope. Listen Johnnie, someone did follow me home, but I couldn't get the plate number. I have my Beretta and I have . . . shit."

Scat jumped on top of the monitor and licked a paw.

"You all right?"

"Yes, damn it. Scat startled me. What a scary cat. Girl or boy?"

"I don't know. I'm not good at that sort of gender thing. You're not mad, are you, Mel?"

"No. I'm not mad, just don't have time. If I can catch him or her when I leave, I'll bring it home for you. Say, how did Scat get inside? All the windows and doors are closed."

"Beats me. I don't have a clue."

"Want some news?"

"Shoot."

"Our client was born Peter Connelly. He has a mother who doesn't know he's dead. He underwent extensive plastic surgery to change his identity by a Dr. Sarah Reynolds. Is she a piece of work? Changed his name to Paul Cooper. The real Paul Cooper was killed on his prom night. He was seventeen. Peter obtained Paul's ID, ordered a new birth certificate, and assumed the deceased's entire life."

"So, he's hiding from something?"

"Or someone?"

"Or both?"

"Here's the NCIC update. He robbed the Western Guaranty Bank in Los Angeles. I have the FBI Website on-line now and just e-mailed them asking for the Agent-in-Charge or someone to contact me about this case."

"Damn. New problems."

"Not the least of which is the torn bond he gave us. Came from that bank. Remember?"

"Well, there goes our fee."

"Don't be so pessimistic."

"Not negative. Just careful, like you should be."

"And then . . ."

"And you're taking a chance letting the FBI know this guy is dead. 'Cause X-Ray doesn't know it yet. Maybe they'll call him, and you'll get in trouble with the chief again."

"I'm not telling them he's dead. I'm merely interested in an old case because when my dad died, I 'found' this old bearer bond from that bank Peter robbed. I'm naturally nosy and want to know more about it."

"Shit," Johnnie muffled his reply.

"Are the sheets over your head again?"

"Yep."

"Good. Stay there and we'll pick you up on our way home."

"We?"

"Yeah. Me, Scat and the bad guy who's following us."

"Shit." Johnnie hung up.

❖ Chapter 12 ❖

"FBI Special Agent Jack House speaking. You had some questions about an old case of mine?"

"Yes, thank you Special Agent House. See, I have this old bearer bond from the Western Guaranty Bank in L.A., and I happened to see an old case about the robbery at that bank."

"Not one of my better victories, I'm afraid."

"Why's that?"

"We never recovered the money."

"Then the bond I have may not be good?"

"Oh, I didn't say that. Just that all the currency stolen was never recovered."

"How much did they get?"

"Over two hundred fifty thousand dollars."

"Wow. Lots of bucks."

"Interesting story goes with it."

"I've got time. I'd love to hear it," Mel said.

"This was an inside job. Peter Connelly was a loan officer. Banks don't pay decent salaries, as a rule. Some consider it a license to steal. Anyway, Peter's story is a sad one. His wife was killed and his ten-year-old daughter seriously injured in a car accident."

"Hmm."

"What Peter told us when we caught him . . . was the other driver had no insurance and his finances quickly ran out. His little girl had a closed head . . . a kind of brain injury . . . and was in a coma until she died several years later."

"I understand. I lost my own son to a hit-and-run driver."

"Sorry about your loss. Anyway, Peter put her in a rehab-type hospital, sold the family home, and liquidated his assets. He was under a great deal of stress. Suffered with horrible migraines, followed by long absences from work, so the bank officials placed him on probation. Peter rented a toilet of an apartment, and that's where he met a guy, a neighbor named . . . Buddy Danko, who worked at a nightclub. I forget which one."

"Is Buddy his real name?"

"Yeah. You're challenging my memory, Miss Walker. As I recall, he used other aka's, but Buddy was his real first name."

"Did he have a record?"

"Mostly petty stuff, B & E, possession . . ."

"Okay. Breaking and entering. Drug possession?"

"No. Arms."

"He carries a weapon?"

"Known to, yeah."

"How did Peter and Buddy get so tight?"

"Buddy invited Peter over for free drinks. I remember now. The bar was called the Skin Inn . . . in Costa Mesa, off Harbor Boulevard."

"Sounds like a strip joint."

"Big time. Lots of drugs and rock-n-roll. Then over time, this nice accountant-type guy and his bouncer-bud get pretty tight. Soon they're ragging on about their jobs. One night he and Buddy got drunk, comparing bosses and how life sucked. And how one big heist would set them up for life."

"And because Peter's daughter had incurred so many medical expenses, he was particularly vulnerable."

"Right."

"So Peter, who had the keys to the vault so to speak, gets pulled into the scheme."

"Yeah."

"But you caught them?" Mel asked.

"It didn't take a genius to identify the disgruntled employee. He'd been writing threatening letters to the personnel department demanding reinstatement. He wasn't that strong."

"Did you give him a plea?"

"Yeah. Like the local cops, we deal. It was a 'note-job,' that is to say, the teller didn't see any weapon, just a hand-written note from Buddy."

"So a 'note-job' receives less time than a what . . . 'weapon-job'?"

"Yeah, generally. So we got Peter for six years. Buddy did eight. Both served roughly eighty percent of their time. Peter's been out almost a year. Buddy just paroled."

"Where were they incarcerated? Susanville?"

"No, as a matter of fact. I believe Peter was kept locally."

"Here? Where? I didn't know we had a unit."

"The Metro Detention Center . . . MDC we call it."

"I don't think I ever heard of that unit. Where is it?"

"Right behind the Roybal Center in downtown L.A. You've probably passed it a hundred times. It's a high-rise building. Has small windows with bars on them."

"That's rather confining."

"The prisoners keep busy. They have jobs and responsibilities just like every other institution."

"Special Agent House, you have me really curious. You said

you found some of the money?"

"Some loose change. But not the big stuff. Peter told us he never had possession of it . . . that Buddy double-crossed him."

"And you believed Peter?"

"We never developed any evidence that he ever had the money in his possession after Buddy split. He had no bank accounts, no new car . . . not a pot or a window, if you know what I mean."

"Is Peter still on probation?"

"Probably."

"What's the status on your case? About the money, I mean."

"The file's closed."

"You didn't go after the money?"

"Miss Walker, Los Angeles is the bank-robbery capital of the world. As a representative of the FBI, I've been interviewed over four hundred times. I'm going to tell you what I tell the reporters; it's a case of too many robberies and too few manpower hours."

"Maybe there'd be a reward for the money. That is, if it's ever found."

"The bank may offer a reward. I don't know about that."

"So. No matter what happens to Peter Connelly or that Buddy Danko, your case is still closed?"

"I have no interest in it at all, Miss Walker."

"I really appreciate your taking time to talk with me. I never realized you guys would be so forthcoming and prompt. Thanks a lot."

"You're welcome. You have my direct line in case you have any other questions?"

"Yes, thanks. I was thinking, in the event I might want to read the complete file, and I can't imagine that I would, is there a way for me to see the paperwork on this robbery?"

"Sure. Under the Freedom of Information Act, you can go to the federal clerk's office in downtown Los Angeles. You can see anything we submitted into evidence."

"And that would include statements given by Connelly and Danko?"

"If we introduced them into the record, yes. Again, I've investigated more than four hundred bank robberies. I have no idea what's in each court file."

"Oh sure, I understand that. Well, thanks again."

"Good luck in your search."

Mel hung up the phone, put on her Sam Browne belt, and shoved the gun in the holster. She cut off the computer, snatched the sleeping cat, and locked the house behind her.

Scat bawled an agonized wail and paced back and forth across the back seat.

"Scat, I know how you feel," Mel said. She scanned her rearview mirror for the now familiar dark sedan.

At the hospital Mel pulled a jacket from the trunk and put it on over the gun and holster. "Scat, you stay here. I'll be right back with Johnnie."

Mel walked into Johnnie's room to find him fussing with his clothing.

"Hi. Need some help with that zipper?"

"No. I definitely don't." He turned away from Mel.

"Oh, come on, you don't have anything I haven't seen a hundred times before. Let me help you."

Johnnie turned, stared at the ceiling, and rolled his eyes.

"That's nothing to brag about. Okay, I won't look . . . so just do it."

She bent to one knee. "First of all, you have your shirttail caught in it." She tugged at the zipper tab and tried to dislodge the trapped material.

"Oh, this is a great scene," X-Ray said, as he entered the room. "What do we have here?"

Johnnie raised his left hand to his face, "Oh, that's just great. A cop catches me with my pants down and you on your knees facing my crotch."

Mel laughed so hard she fell off balance and landed on the floor bumping her butt. X-Ray joined in the laughter.

"That is not funny. That is definitely not funny." Johnnie placed his left hand on his hip and turned away. "I'm feeling very vulnerable right now, my arm hurts, and I can't zip up my pants."

"Oh, Johnnie, I'm sorry. We're not laughing at you. Here, let me help." Mel got on her knees again and crawled around in front of Johnnie. A few seconds of muffled giggles later, she freed the zipper.

"I thought I'd drop by and check on you," X-Ray said. "But it looks like Mel has everything well in hand."

X-Ray, Johnnie and Mel giggled at the pun.

"We're going to be fine," Mel said. "I'm taking him home to Rosa. She'll mother him to pieces."

"She definitely isn't going to zip up my pants." Johnnie carried his razor and deodorant to a small plastic bag the nurse had given him.

"Let me help you," X-Ray said, as he stuffed the toiletries in the kit, then tucked it under his arm. "Okay, are we ready?"

"You need to ride with me," Mel told Johnnie. She and X-Ray walked down the aisle to the exit door. An attendant pushed

Johnnie's wheelchair. "I have Scat, and he ... or she ... is having a fit. I just pray it hasn't scratched the leather seats."

"Scat?" X-Ray asked.

"I found him in the office one morning. I don't have any idea how he got inside the house. He was pacing up and down in the kitchen, making the most painful sounds you ever heard. I fed it. Told it to scat ... shoo ... go away. He said he liked the name Scat and stayed," Johnnie said.

"And all this happened while I was on vacation?"

"A day or so after you left. Like your dad might have sent him, you know, to watch over us?"

"Don't start that. Cats and I don't always agree. And this one definitely doesn't like me," Mel said.

"Well, he loves me and he won't be in your way. I promise."

"Can we keep him? Huh? Huh?" X-Ray pleaded.

"Oh, grow up, both of you silly idiots." Mel opened the passenger's door to find Scat sitting calmly on the front seat. "Jesus. Is that a smile?"

"Looks like a smile," X-Ray said. "He's really glad to see you, Johnnie."

"Come here, my new little buddy." Johnnie scooped Scat up and placed the cat inside his arm sling.

"Good grief." Mel slammed the door and pointed at Johnnie as she walked around the car with X-Ray. "And that's a grown man."

"Another reason I stopped by was to let you know the fingerprints came back. Thought I'd let you know who your client is, or rather was?"

Mel climbed into the driver's seat and said just before closing her door, "Oh, you mean Peter Connelly, bank robber extraordinaire?"

❖ Chapter 13 ❖

X-Ray stood with his mouth open and his hands on his hips, as Mel backed from the parking space and drove down the aisle to the exit.

"Oh, is he pissed off," Johnnie said, as he stroked Scat who rewarded him with a purr.

"You mean that I might have suppressed evidence?"

"Might? How about altered, hidden, moved, touched, and violated?"

"Don't be so harsh. He'll get over it."

"Will we live long enough to see that, Scat?" Johnnie asked, nuzzling the cat's face. "Oh, it's going to be so cold in that dark dungeon X-Ray will send us to."

"We may not make it that far," Mel replied.

"Wha . . .?"

"I think Buddy Danko is following us."

"Who's Buddy Danko?"

Mel sped down Pacific Coast Highway and watched her rear-view mirror. By the time they reached her private gate, she had told

68

Johnnie everything she learned from the FBI. Mel drove the car into the resident's lane, hit the gate buzzer, and sped through, leaving the dark sedan behind.

Johnnie turned in his seat. "Well, he's not getting through that gate. But, there's always the beach."

She patted her rib area, "And there's always Lady Beretta."

"Good grief." He sank into the seat. "You have no active permit, just met with Harbour Pointe's top cop, and you're packing. Lord help us, Scat."

"Johnnie, you worry too much. Hmm, you're right about the beach. We aren't a fortress. I have work to do, and I don't like leaving you here, with or without Rosa. You can't shoot with your left hand, can you?"

"I can barely shoot with my good one."

"That's because you don't practice like I do."

"I don't like the sounds."

"Pussy."

Scat cocked his head sideways and said, "Purr."

Mel pulled into the circular driveway and honked the horn. Rosa opened both front doors and rushed out. When Rosa saw Scat, she stopped. "Here, let me help you with . . . what is that?"

"Scat," Mel said, as she came around the car

"Oh, I love cats. Come here, sweet baby." Rosa took Scat from Johnnie's arm sling and walked back into the house, leaving Mel to help Johnnie out of the car.

"This is going to be fun. You, Rosa, and Scat versus me."

"Scat adores you."

"Right."

"Welcome home, Johnnie," Rosa said.

"Will Mel be okay about me using Willie's room?"

"It was her idea. Right?"

"Right," Mel answered, as she entered the room and looked at the bed."

"Good. That's settled. I have dinner for you. And X-Ray has called here every ten minutes asking for you. Said your car phone was not on, and he urgently needs to talk with you."

"Rosa, you smell like chocolate," Johnnie said.

"I made you cocoa *empanadas* for dessert. There are fresh sheets on the bed and clean towels in the bath. I'll be back for breakfast. Okay?"

"Fine," Mel said. "One thing you must promise me, Rosa."

"What?"

"If you are followed by anyone, or suspect you're being followed, go straight to the police department. Do not go home, and don't come back here."

Rosa wiped her hands on the apron, shook her head, and left the room. "*Madre Mia.* I'm going to die tonight."

Mel caught up to Rosa and put her arm around her shoulder. "You're not going to die or even get hurt. I just think there's lots of wackos out there, and I don't want you in any danger. Want me to call X-Ray for an escort?"

Rosa's eyes danced, "Will X-Ray come himself?"

"Probably not. But Harbour Pointe does have some new stud-muffin cadets who might interest you."

"Oh, you're such a tease. I'll be careful. See you tomorrow."

Rosa picked up her purse at the front door and called out, "Johnnie, get some sleep, and I'll see you in the morning."

"Bye, Rosa," Johnnie hollered.

Scat brushed against Rosa's ankle as she reached the front door. "And don't forget to feed the kitty when you two eat. He's beautiful. We're going to keep him?"

"Yes. I guess we will." The phone rang, and Mel picked up the receiver in her small study. "Hello, Walker residence."

"Okay, so how did you know who your client was?" X-Ray demanded.

"I was just going to call you. We got home and Johnnie is . . ."

"That's not what I asked you."

"I'm stalling."

"Oh, the truth would be nice. That way you don't have to remember the lie."

"Truth, huh? What a concept." Johnnie walked past the office door with Scat following close behind. Mel heard Johnnie talking to Scat about being hungry. She spoke slowly, creating her answer as she went. "I knew . . . my client . . . was . . . Peter . . . Connelly . . . because . . ."

A loud crash stopped her cold.

Johnnie's shaky voice called out to her, "Mel, can you come here, please?"

She took the cordless phone and rushed to him. "Are you okay?"

"Don't ask that. Last time you did, I got shot," Johnnie replied.

A voice that sounded familiar to her said, "I'm not going to kill you. I just want my money."

❖ Chapter 14 ❖

When Mel entered the living room, Johnnie's good arm was in the air, his eyes wide, as he faced a mountain of a man holding a large black revolver.

"Raise your hands and come here," the man demanded.

Remember what he looks like, she thought. She took inventory and slowly walked toward him. Male. White. Mid-'30s. Six-foot-three, two hundred twenty plus pounds. Clean shaven. Jeans, T-shirt, tennis shoes. Weight-lifter body. Blond hair, long at the back and tied with something. Receding hairline over a small, round head. A small gold earring in a right earlobe. Large blue eyes with bushy eyebrows that almost meet at the top of a bulbous nose and thick lips. A tattoo of something on the right forearm. Right-handed.

"Whatever you say, Buddy Danko," she bellowed, still holding the phone near her face. "Why didn't you ring the doorbell? Now I've got a dining room slider to replace. Look at all this broken glass." Mel chattered, hoping X-Ray heard her and understood the urgency.

"How'd you know my name?"

"The FBI told me."

"Shut up lady, and get over here. Put down the phone."

Mel placed the receiver face up on the dining room table and followed his instructions.

"What do you want with us?" she asked.

"I want the money Peter gave you."

"He didn't give us any money." Mel added, "He hired us to do something for him, but you killed him before he got a chance to tell us what it was."

"I never killed anybody." The gun shook in his hand.

"Okay. Let's shelve the question of who killed Peter for a minute. Try to get it through your thick skull, Danko. Any missing money is a surprise to us," Mel said.

"What are you saying?"

"Peter told the FBI you had it and hid it from him."

"That's a damn lie." Danko pointed the gun at her.

Johnnie said, "Mel, please don't piss this guy off."

"The truth can't hurt anyone. Isn't that right? Want to know why Peter didn't serve as much time in prison as you did? He told the FBI you had the money. That's why he couldn't return it."

"I never touched the dough after we left the bank. Peter said he knew the safest place for the money. We split up, and next thing I know, we were arrested."

"Then why did you kill him?"

"I told you, lady, I didn't kill him. I didn't know he was dead till you just now told me."

"If you were such good friends, why didn't you just go and ask him for your share, then?" Johnnie asked.

"Because I thought he'd given it to you guys already."

"Why would you think that?" Mel asked.

"Peter told me he'd given it to you for safekeeping."

Mel shook her head. "Peter lied to you and to the FBI."

"The first time we ever met him was the night you shot him; or rather he got shot," Johnnie corrected himself. "And we didn't have much time to talk, if you know what I mean?" He motioned to his bandaged arm.

"Fuck." Buddy lowered the gun, eased down on the arm of the living room sofa, and stared out the window toward the ocean below.

Both Mel and Johnnie put their arms slowly down, but did not rush him.

"Well, where the fuck is it?" Buddy demanded, his angry eyes darting between Mel and Johnnie.

"We don't know," she said.

Inside the house, no one spoke. Outside, the only noises were the palm fronds whispering against each other in the breeze. The solitary thing she would remember later when the ringing in her ears went away and she could hear again, was the scream of flash bangs as diversionary bombs filled the air with smoke. The house shuddered under the assault.

A dozen men wearing black hoods and goggles and carrying AK47's with laser sights, charged through the smoke-filled home and shouted, "Harbour Pointe Police. Get down!"

"Throw out your weapons and lie down."

"Do not move. Lie on your stomach."

"Put your hands behind your head."

A strong arm shoved Mel to the floor. She rolled onto her stomach and placed both hands behind her head. Sweat filled the air. There was the kind of odor caused by nervous sweat when adrenaline runs hard and fast through a cop's veins: strong and musky. Her heart pounded so strong she felt the beat against the carpet. She waited to be addressed.

"Mel, are you okay?"

"Johnnie, I'm fine. And you?"

"Sore. I got pushed."

"Ditto."

The police opened the front door. The other section of the slider glass had shattered from the explosives. A draft pulled by the ocean breezes cleared the vapor from the living area.

Mel heard coughing behind her, but did not move. Her mouth dry, she tried to swallow.

Two rough arms took each of her hands and jerked her to a standing position. Mel looked at the chests of the two SWAT members dressed in black and said, "Thanks for the infantry."

They pulled their dark goggles and hoods to the top of their heads and took a deep breath. Both stood well over six-foot five-inches, and their combined weights would have qualified them as defensive backs for the Dallas Cowboys.

She looked up and added, "If I ever need bodyguards I know who to call."

"No problem," they replied.

"Mel, you better quit calling us, period," X-Ray suggested. "This is not good."

"I know. You don't know how sorry I am about all this."

One of the SWAT members helped Johnnie to his feet.

"Are you hurt?" Mel said.

"No. Just more sore, thank you very much. And being pushed to the floor wasn't fun either."

"Not intended to be fun. If he decided to shoot, I needed both of you out of the range of fire."

"Don't think we aren't grateful. We are, aren't we, Mel?" Johnnie asked.

"Grateful enough to tell the truth?" X-Ray asked.

"I don't know if I'd go that far. Let's catch our breaths first," she said.

Mel filled glasses of water for Johnnie and herself and

returned to the living room. Three officers stood on either side of Buddy Danko. Two policemen placed handcuffs on him, while the third one asked Buddy questions and wrote on a notepad.

"Your real name is . . .?"

"Buddy Danko."

"No middle name?"

"No, boss man."

"Buddy is real?"

"Yes, sir, boss man."

"Who's your probation officer?"

"His card is in my wallet, sir." Buddy twisted sideways, so his rear pocket would be closer to the officer's grasp.

"You aren't carrying any needles or anything that would stick me, are you?"

"No, sir. I ain't on drugs."

They removed his wallet and pulled out a white piece of paper.

One policeman patted Buddy's body, front and back, and turned each pocket inside out to reveal its emptiness. Another removed Buddy's shoes, shook them, and ran his hands around Buddy's ankles.

"He's clean," one man said, as he placed Buddy's weapon in a brown paper bag, folded the top, and wrote something on it.

"You must be on something, Danko," X-Ray said.

"Why you say that, sir?" Buddy asked. He stared at the floor.

"This lady," pointing to Mel, "is a personal friend of the police department. We don't want anything to ever happen to her. Is that clear?" X-Ray stepped within inches of Buddy's face and spittle flew out on the word, "clear."

"Yes, boss."

"And if we ever hear of you or any of your friends or associates

77

bothering her or this gentleman with the sling on his arm again, your family will need a metal detector to locate all your body parts."

"Loud and clear, sir," Buddy replied faintly.

"Take him in and I'll be along. I have a lot more questions for Mel."

The lead officer nodded at X-Ray, pulled a card from inside his coat and began to read, "You have the right to remain silent," and the three policemen escorted Buddy through the front door to a waiting patrol unit.

❖ Chapter 15 ❖

"You knew your client's name was Peter Connelly because ... ?" X-Ray asked.

Mel, Johnnie, and X-Ray were seated at the breakfast room table. X-Ray held a pad of paper and a pen poised to take notes.

"The FBI told me," Mel said.

"What?"

"After I found out who my client was, I ran him on NCIC. I called the local FBI office and spoke with Peter's arresting officer. He filled me in on the bank robbery."

"I thought you knew who he was when you moved his car to Bernie's parking lot the night he was killed."

"What car?" Mel asked.

"I'll get us some more hot tea. Would anyone like cookies with that tea?" Johnnie asked.

"No cookies."

"Okay, so I created a little information slowdown for you."

X-Ray slammed his fist on the table and stared at her. "Mel, you tampered with evidence."

"How'd you know it was me who moved the car?"

"You just told me." He slapped the table again, stood up, and walked to the door leading onto the rear deck.

"Shit." Mel got up and joined Johnnie in the kitchen. He

placed three cups of tea and a small plate of cookies on a wooden tray. She picked up the tray and followed Johnnie back to the table. "Okay, you got me."

X-Ray returned to the table. "Good. Now, the truth. The car was registered in the name of Peter Connelly. How'd you get to Paul Cooper from Peter Connelly?"

"Same initials?"

"I don't think your dad would appreciate that cute remark. You've already lost your permit to carry a weapon for sixty days. I had to save your life tonight. Don't put your investigator's license and our friendship on the line."

"You're right. Dad didn't raise me like that." Mel slumped in a chair, took a deep breath, and continued, "I traced Paul Cooper and found out he was dead. I realized Peter went to great pains to take on a new identification. I found his keys and went to his house to check it out. Peter has a mother. I talked with her. She doesn't know he's dead. We need to notify her."

"From inside his home, you called his mother?"

Mel toyed with her hair with one hand and rolled the edges of a paper napkin with the other. "Yes."

"We could add breaking and entering to charges mounting against you," X-Ray said. "What were you thinking? Did you take anything?"

"No," Mel added. "Oops, yeah I did."

"You didn't tell me," Johnnie said.

"What evidence did you take?" X-Ray shouted.

"A key. I found a key frozen to the bottom of a package in the freezer." She stood, patted her jeans' pocket, pulled out a key, and handed it to X-Ray. "I think it must fit a safety-deposit box somewhere."

X-Ray turned the key over in his palm. "Yep, that's what it

looks like."

"I told her specifically not to get involved," Johnnie said, and waved his left palm back and forth, face-out.

"I was going to give it to you."

"When?"

"Today, probably. You have the authority to get into the boxes and that's where Peter must have hid the money from Buddy. Before you came in, Buddy said Peter told him the loot was in a safe place. That'd be ironic, you know? They stole the money from a bank and then hid it in a bank."

"You don't think Buddy killed him?" X-Ray asked.

"I thought his voice sounded familiar when I first heard it. Now, I'm not so sure. Anyway, we faced his loaded gun, our lives were in his hands, and he didn't shoot us. Why would Buddy lie to us? What did he have to lose?" Mel asked.

"We were no threat to him," Johnnie added.

"That's true," X-Ray agreed. "Do you have the note Peter sent you?"

"Yeah, I do." She took her car keys and disappeared down the hall to the garage. Moments later she returned carrying the note, the bond, and the envelope.

X-Ray studied it for a moment, then spoke. "So he hired you to do something and you don't know what?"

"Exactly," Johnnie replied for them.

"What is this?" X-Ray asked. He turned the bond over and read the back.

"Part of our fee."

"It's from the Western Guaranty Bank. When you put both halves together, you get a negotiable ten thousand dollar bearer bond," Mel said.

"Where's the other piece?"

"We don't know," Johnnie answered.

"What we're hoping is that the money from the bank robbery is in the safety-deposit box along with the other side of this. Maybe the box holds other secrets too. Like who had a motive to kill Peter, and why he wanted to hire us." Mel looked from Johnnie to X-Ray.

"Okay. So I'll get a search warrant. In the meantime, you are not, I repeat, not to work on this case until you hear from me again." X-Ray gave each of them a hard look.

"I stand admonished," Mel agreed.

"Me too," Johnnie shook his head, placed his hand over his heart and held up three fingers.

"I'll have one of my men pick up some plyboard so you can secure the house tonight," X-Ray said.

"Thanks."

After dinner she swept up the shards of glass and placed pieces of plyboard against the slider opening. "That'll have to do until we can get some glass guys here in the morning."

Mel sat at the computer with her chin propped on her fist. She tapped the keyboard with the other hand. Johnnie sipped his coffee, sat in a chair next to the desk, and looked over her shoulder.

"What are you doing?" Johnnie asked.

"Checking on Danko's record."

"I gave my Boy Scout honor we'd stay out of this."

"You were never a Boy Scout."

"How'd you know?" He sat upright.

"You just told me."

Johnnie snapped his fingers. "Damn."

"Just how X-Ray caught me."

Mel clicked the Print key and turned to the copier on the credenza behind her.

"Bad guy?" Johnnie asked.

"Long record. But, like the FBI agent said, mostly breaking and entering. Small-time hoodlum stuff."

Mel turned the papers at an angle so Johnnie could read with her.

"There's our bank robbery," Johnnie pointed. "Did they have any other accomplices? Somebody else who knew about the heist?"

"Like the FBI suggested, we'll have to take the file numbers on these cases to the Federal Court in L.A. to look at the physical documents."

"I'd like to help. Why don't I check the criminal records in Santa Ana? I'll take the hand-held recorder since I can't write."

"Look for anything we can use."

"Accomplices, associates, friends, relatives."

"Anyone with a motive and opportunity."

"Copy any reports we may need."

"Sure. When are we going to the Skin Inn?" Johnnie asked.

"Thought I'd start there early tomorrow morning."

"Before L.A.?"

"I certainly want that freeway parking lot to L.A. to clear before I start that journey."

"What do you think the Skin Inn looks like?" Johnnie asked.

"You're asking me? What makes you think I'd know?"

Johnnie stood with his weight on one hip. "And you think I'm an expert?"

"Well, I can guess. It's grimy, smoky, and dark. Music pounding the eardrums, naked bodies sweating, and diluted drinks flowing. Not a nice place for a lady to be seen. Wanna go with me?" Mel grinned.

Johnnie turned his head and listened, then ran out of the study toward the back patio. "Oh, my God, Scat. Scat, where are you?"

"Oh, shit," Mel ran after Johnnie. "We forgot about Scat."

❖ Chapter 16 ❖

A blood-curdling scream that began as a high-pitched wail shocked Mel awake. She pulled off her eyeshade and scrambled out of bed. "Rosa, are you okay?" she hollered.

Johnnie called back, "Don't ask. I'm on the case."

Mel heard footsteps running through the house. She slipped a robe over her nightshirt, then ran down the stairs taking them two risers at a time.

Rosa stood beside the sofa, her hands to the side of her face. Johnnie reached her before Mel cleared the bottom stairway.

"What's the matter?" Johnnie asked.

"Virgin Mary! Look at this." Rosa pointed to the slider.

"It's just plywood," Johnnie said.

"What happened?"

Mel put her arm around Rosa's shoulder. "We, Johnnie and I, accidentally broke the glass last night. It's no big deal."

"Yeah. That's all," Johnnie added.

Rosa looked at Johnnie and Mel. "You big liars. You never broke this."

"Oh, yes, we did. That's exactly what happened."

Johnnie nodded. "It was an accident. We broke it so late last night we just laid boards against the opening. We planned on calling a glass shop this morning."

Rosa sniffed. "Well, if that's what happened . . . then, we're not in trouble. Are you sure?"

"Scout's honor," Johnnie and Mel smiled, each holding three fingers in the air.

"My cousin Hector, he knows a glazier. He will have it fixed." Rosa looked at the floor in the kitchen. "Where's Scat? You didn't put out fresh food and water for him."

"Well, that's the other news," Mel said.

"When we," Johnnie pointed to himself and Mel, "broke the glass; the confusion and noise scared Scat and he ran away."

"We looked for him a long time," Mel said, her hands behind her back, fingers crossed.

"I'm devastated," Johnnie added. "But he'll come home when he's hungry."

"We'd spend more time looking for him this morning, but Johnnie and I have appointments."

"First, I'll fix breakfast," Rosa said. "Then, I'll bathe Johnnie."

"Help me, Mel. Help me," were the last words she heard as she closed the garage door behind her and drove onto Pacific Coast Highway.

❖ Chapter 17 ❖

The Skin Inn parking lot had a fresh coat of black asphalt and, according to a portable sign, provided valet parking after six-o'clock. The boxy, one-story building might pass for an industrial warehouse, but for the shiny aluminum stripes, hot pink columns, and neon lights.

Mel circled the area twice before a large black four-by-four vacated a spot. She applied new lipstick, exited the car, and tucked her shirttail into the back side of her jean waistband before entering the dimly lit bar.

Hard-rock noise from a stereo system assailed her ears and thick wisps from a floral cleanser caught in her throat.

Jesus, the place is full, she thought. Mel's eyes adjusted to the darkness as she squinted at her watch. Eight-thirty in the morning. Get a job.

A bosomy bartender wearing a white, crocheted halter looked up from behind the bar and fixed her sad, faded-brown eyes on Mel. The woman wore black shorts cut high over her rear-end. Frayed ends of her hard-bleached yellow hair flowed like static around her frail face. Each ear had four or five piercings and none of the dangling rings matched. The bar towel she used slowed to a light swirl when she spotted the newcomer.

"Hi, honey. Lookin' for a job?"

Mel looked down at her own breasts and smiled. "That's a nice compliment. No thanks. I'm looking for the boss. Is he in?"

"Terry? At this time of day? You gotta be kiddin'. He won't be here 'til probably four or four-thirty."

A heavyset, long-jowled man biting a cigarette butt swirled his barstool around to face Mel. "What'd ya want Terry for? You sellin' advertisements?"

"No, not exactly."

Mel scanned the room filled with men. Their focus was a large stage that featured a runway and two brass poles separated by a matching brass railing. She estimated the men's ages ranged from thirty to seventy. Some smoked, despite the no-smoking ordinance. And all drank beer from long necks.

The man at the bar snarled, "If you ain't lookin' for a job, and you ain't selling anythin', what are you here for?"

She crossed the black-and-confetti colored carpet and approached the end of the bar, the brightest area in the room. Mel laid a hand on the bar and sat on an empty stool. The floral odor that overpowered her when she first entered now became a subtle combination of fragrances.

"I need to talk with whoever hired Buddy Danko. Would that be Terry?"

The bartender wiped her hands on a towel wrapped around her tiny waist and approached Mel. A gaunt, almost anorexic childlike body accompanied those cheerless eyes.

"I don't know that anyone actually hired that asshole," she said. "He was a regular here for years. Then one day we had a bit of a problem; Buddy beat the crap outta a guy . . . a regular customer . . . and we threw him out."

The smoker dragged on his cigarette, coughed, and added, "I guess we just adopted him." He extended his right hand. "My name's Sam."

Mel shook his hand. "Mine's Camellia."

"What do ya need him for?" the bartender asked.

"Oh, I don't need him. As a matter of fact, I saw him last night."

Both Sam and the bartender gave each other sardonic glances as Mel added, "I want to talk about the bank robbery he served some prison time for."

"Are you a cop?" Sam asked, as he leaned forward.

"She don't look like a cop," the bartender added.

"No. I'm not a police officer. I'm an investigator. And, an old friend of his is in trouble and asked me to look him up."

Sam relaxed. "Okay. You ain't a cop. Let's see if we can help you. What can I get you to drink?"

"It's a little early for . . ."

"Are you refusing to drink with me?" he asked, eyeing her again.

"No. No. Not at all. A cola would be good. Anything diet. Is that okay?"

"Sure, honey," the bartender smiled and replied, as she reached into a silver cooler filled with ice. "Sam here is just teasing you. He's probably the best one to answer questions 'bout Buddy. They used to be roommates, Miss ah . . ."

"Outside or inside prison?" She propped her feet on the brass rail, both elbows against the counter edge, and added, "My friends call me Mel."

"I knew him in prison and here at the bar. Is you a dyke?" Sam asked.

"No. Real name's Camellia Walker. But everyone calls me Mel."

"Okay, Mel. Shoot. What can I tell you that Buddy wouldn't

already share with you, since you is such good friends and all?" He smiled at the bartender.

Mel took a swallow. "How long have you known Buddy?"

Sam stared at the mirror behind the bar. The music ended and another song, louder and more abrasive than the first, began to play. The lights dimmed and the men behind her clapped. "We met at MDC."

"The federal pen downtown L.A.?"

"Yeah."

"Know him to have any close friends? Or family?"

"Never got no letters that I knew about. No visitors either, come to think of it." He scratched his salt-and-pepper hair. White puffs of dandruff flew into the air and landed on his plaid work-shirt.

"Now, Buddy tells me he and another dude planned that job."

"Yeah." He turned and pointed to a series of pink-vinyl circular booths against one wall. "They did the plan right here. Put it on paper and even asked my advice. He and Peter Connelly, a banker type, they was tight." Sam held up two fingers pressed together. "And with Peter doin' the inside bank thing, and Buddy the note and the getaway . . . well . . . that's all they needed."

"So you know Peter?"

"Quiet little guy. Bad shit happened to him ought not to happen to anybody, losing his wife and baby girl like that." He shook his head and mashed the cigarette butt into the bottom of an overflowing ashtray.

If you only knew the really bad shit, Mel thought.

"Sam, it's Charlotte," the bartender motioned behind him.

He spun his stool toward the mirrored stage. "Sh-h," he said. "This is mine and Buddy's gal."

Mel turned her stool around. Jesus, she thought. Her eyes wide.

***

Charlotte undulated in sensual movements that reminded Mel of clothes lurching over and over in a dryer. Her waist-length strawberry-colored hair swished around her buxom body as she removed each piece of clothing. Her breasts played hide and seek with the hair, until Charlotte wore only a tired smile and a small flesh-colored G-string.

I'm exhausted, Mel thought. I don't get that much exercise in a month.

She spun the stool to face the bar and picked up her cola. Sam looked like a forlorn orphan awaiting his last meal. When the music ended, he clapped wildly, put a thumb and index finger in his mouth, and whistled. He waved at Charlotte and she blew him a kiss. Sam sighed and looked at Mel.

"You were askin'?"

"I wondered if he had any friends or family. Anybody he would trust?"

"Nobody, lessen it'd be Charlotte, maybe."

"Did he have a lot of money after the robbery?" Mel asked.

Both Sam and the bartender laughed so loud the audience turned and looked at them.

"Honey, Buddy didn't have no money. Not before or after the heist," the bartender said.

"I thought they got almost a quarter million dollars," Mel suggested.

"If they did, Buddy never saw any of it after he and Peter walked outta the bank."

91

"Why, Buddy owed this joint a huge bar tab, which Terry took from his last paycheck. I think Buddy cleared about twelve bucks after that," the bartender said.

"Then where do you think all that money went?" Mel asked.

"What money?" came a question from behind Mel.

She turned as Charlotte approached the threesome. She wore a loose see-through robe tied at the neckline.

"Buddy's bank robbery money," Mel answered her. "Where do you think Buddy hid all that money?"

"Got no idea. He told me that other guy Peter took it for safekeeping. Then Buddy was picked up, had a quick trial, was sentenced, and went to prison."

"He didn't give you anything? Like a key?" Mel asked.

"Who are you, anyway?" Charlotte asked.

Mel offered her hand. "I'm Mel Walker. I'm an investigator working on a case. I saw Buddy last night and he told me he didn't know where Peter put the money. But I thought he was just kidding me."

Sam snorted, "Buddy don't kid about money, lady."

"Didn't have a fancy car or apartment? No flash money, or material things?"

"Nope," they all replied in unison.

"As a matter of fact," Charlotte said, "I had to loan him some money this morning."

"Where'd you get the money, if you don't mind my asking?" Mel looked at the dancer.

Charlotte patted her flesh-colored bra and answered, "Right here, lady. Hard work, long hours, and two big tits."

"Thanks for your honest response." Mel took several cards from her wallet and gave one each to the bartender, Sam, and Charlotte, adding, "If you should think of anything else that might help me find the missing money, I'd like to hear from you."

She pulled five dollars from her purse to pay for the drink, but Sam refused her offer. "You helpin' Buddy and Charlotte, this one's on me this time. Come back to see us."

"Thank you, Sam. I appreciate your time and your honesty too . . . all of you." She stuffed the bill in a glass tip jar, winked at the bartender, waved and backed toward the door.

"Let the Good Times Roll" began to play and the next dancer walked on stage.

Wow, was all Mel thought, as she started the engine. She drove the 405 Freeway north past choking diesel fumes, traffic alerts, and orange-cone delineations that altered lane patterns and forced more congestion. All the aggravation interrupted the Johnnie Hooker's blues tape that began, "I woke up this morning."

Ninety minutes later, Mel sighed and pulled into the parking garage near the Los Angeles courthouse.

The cold, damp basement was filled with several acres of metal file cabinets and cardboard banker boxes. Weary civil employees pushed grocery cart-like baskets up and down concrete aisles.

Mel presented her ID. "I'd like to order this file," she said, when her turn came.

"You can look at it over there." The clerk motioned to rows of long metal tables and folding chairs that filled a side room.

"Okay," Mel drummed the counter top and waited for the file. The large-bodied clerk raised both arms and slapped the banker box on the counter, like tossing hay into the back of a flatbed. In a rhythmic chant as if he had said it a thousand times, "If you need copies, fill out this form. We only do twenty-five copies at a time. If you want more than twenty-five, you'll have to leave your request and some money and we'll mail it to you. Takes a couple of days."

Mel lifted the dusty carton, held it to her chest, and walked into the review room.

She found the Register, wrote down the Bates index numbers, and began her search. Mel sifted through the material until she had broken one nail, snagged a cuticle on a loose staple, and paper-cut the inside of one palm.

Mel also found Peter's statement. If he told the FBI the truth, he did not have the money.

Her beeper sounded as she pulled onto the freeway headed back to Harbour Pointe. She pressed the button, did not recognize the number, but returned the call.

"Let us make you beautiful. How can we help?" a lyrical voice asked.

"It'd take a lot to make me beautiful. This is Mel Walker. Someone at this number paged me."

"Oh, yes, Miss Walker. I believe Dr. Reynolds' surgical consultant wanted to speak with you. Just a moment, please."

Barbra Streisand's compact disc offered Mel an opportunity to reach "Higher Ground," as she merged the Mercedes into traffic on the southbound Harbor Freeway.

"Yes, Miss Walker. I'm Dr. Reynolds' assistant. Dr. Reynolds forgot to tell you yesterday that we're offering a free consultation this month. If you're at all worried about those crow's-feet around your eyes, or those age lines on your forehead, this would be a wonderful opportunity to talk with us. All in confidence, of course."

The melodious voice was compelling.

Mel pulled the vanity mirror open, turned her head left and right, then up and down. She patted the underside of her chin, frowned, smiled, and pulled her bangs back from her hairline. "I never thought I'd have those problems, much less need plastic surgery."

"Oh, Miss Walker. We have lots of ladies your age and even younger who want to turn back Father Time."

"Is it painful?"

"How much pain can we endure for the beauty we will share with our loved ones?"

"Hmm. Well, I'm working on a case right now and don't really have a lot of spare time."

"We're just talking about a consultation. You may decide to have no work done. Right now, let's schedule an appointment. What about day after tomorrow? Do you have nine o'clock available?"

"I think so." Mel stared at the ribbons of red taillights ahead of her. "Sure. What have I got to lose?"

"That's the spirit, Miss Walker. So, we'll see you this week. Have a nice day."

Mel placed a call to Johnnie's beeper, and he returned her call immediately.

"So, what did you find out today, Johnnie?"

"Buddy is a small-time hood. A couple of B & E's. One GTA, reduced to joy riding. A few misdemeanors for possession of arms.

You know, Mel, kinda like everything X-Ray is going to charge you with, when he learns what you've been up to."

"Thanks for rubbing it in. Okay, so he stole a car, broke into a few homes, and liked guns. Any cross-references to any known associates?"

"Nope. This guy is a loner."

"Any family listed?"

"There's a half-sister in the Midwest. I wrote down her name and number. Buddy came from a small family in Ohio. Looks like they weren't the 'let's get together and reminisce' type."

"Who posted bond?"

"Same bail company for each offense. Your old friend and nemesis . . ."

"Bob Bailey Bonds," Mel sighed.

"Yep."

"Did you call him?"

"And steal your fun? Are you kidding?"

"Okay. I'll drop by and see Stinky sometime tomorrow."

"What did you find out?"

"Pretty much the same as you. On Peter: his family perished in the auto accident. He had been a faithful bank employee, a loan officer actually, until they died. Then his behavior changed. He became moody . . . drank . . . work and appearance suffered. He certainly wasn't a professional thief.

"The FBI went straight to him as their number one suspect. When they arrested him, he got the first deal and ratted out on Buddy. Peter apparently put the money in hiding. It was never recovered."

"None of the money?" Johnnie asked.

"The FBI agent told me he found some small change in Peter's apartment. Other than that, the bulk of the booty is missing."

"What's the time frame?"

"The file wasn't clear on those dates. I assume the money disappeared between the time he hid it and was sent to prison."

"That would be logical. Can we define it pretty close on dates?"

"Probably. Let's put our heads together tonight and develop some time lines."

"Anyway, Peter assumed Buddy found the bank's money and took it. The FBI gave Peter the shorter of the prison sentences for the usual reasons: no money, first offense, and not likely to do it again. When Peter got out of prison, zap, no spoils."

"Yeah."

"Mel, do you think Peter might have lied about the money being missing before he went to prison?"

"Anything's possible. Let's ask ourselves why he might do that?"

"He wasn't an experienced criminal. But if I had stolen the money and hid it, I'd tell the FBI that the guy with the criminal record had it. That way, when I paroled, I'd still have big bucks to spend."

"That's not a bad theory."

"What else did those two have in common?"

"Nothing at all, except they met at their apartment building and started drinking together at the Skin Inn. Oh, I forgot to ask. How'd that go?"

"Very intimidating, I must say. Though, I was sorta offered a job today."

Johnnie laughed, "Yeah, right."

"I was," Mel paused. "Can I ask you a question, Johnnie?"

"Sure."

"Do you think I have crow's-feet?" The static from the phone reception crackled.

"What?" Johnnie asked. "I missed that. You found a crow?"

"No. Never mind. I'm on the 405 Freeway coming home. How about dinner?"

"Only if we eat out."

"Afraid Rosa will bathe you before dinner?"

"Never again, Mel. Never again. I'm raw in places I didn't know I had."

"Pussy. How about Mexican food?"

"T.J.'s?"

"See you there."

What a crappy day. I have gray hair, may need plastic surgery, and a quarter of a million dollars is somewhere waiting to be found. Where is the money?

❖ Chapter 18 ❖

T.J.'s, located in the Back Bay behind Newport Beach, sits precariously on a pier supported by aged wooden pilings. Named for longtime owner Tom Jones, the restaurant remains Orange County's best-kept secret. Tom and his wife, Dorothea, serve inexpensive portions of spicy, authentic Mexican food.

Mel pulled into the parking lot and walked to the landing. Johnnie stood at the top of the platform. She joined him, leaned on a railing, and stared at the orange-and-pink sunset forming over the mountains just beyond the estuary waters.

"I'm glad we're eating early. Did you put our names in?" Mel asked.

"Yeah."

"I haven't been here since the night X-Ray told me that Dad left me some money."

"He waited until getting you in public to tell you?" Johnnie asked.

"Yeah. Saved it, for fear I was somehow involved in the illegal activity with Dad."

"Bullshit," Johnnie said.

Johnnie's name was called and they entered the small dining room whose plank floor creaked when they stepped across it.

Dorothea directed them to a window table-for-two, dropped

the menus in front of them, and left to seat another couple.

"What'd you do all day about . . . you know . . . going to the bathroom with your arm in that sling?"

"Elastic." He pulled at the pants and let them snap back against his body. "Wish I'd invented it."

"No shit."

"Works for me."

"That's all that counts. Want a drink?"

"Can't dance. Let's drink."

Dorothea's green eyes turned down at the outer edges. Her mouth a perennial grimace, even when closed. Railroad tracks traversed the hills and valleys of her weary face.

"The usual? *Dos Equis?*" she asked, and pushed a strand of lifeless salt-and-pepper hair off her forehead. Her other hand swiped the tabletop with a damp rag.

"Fine," Johnnie replied.

"Dorothea, do you mind my asking you, your age? Is that too personal?" Mel asked.

"It ain't too personal, Mel. You must'a forgot. You and I have the same month. I'm two years older, that's all. Remember that time T-Bone bought a cake, and you all sang 'Happy Birthday' to me?"

"Right. I forgot. He told you he had two birthdays that month."

"Sure did. Nice fellow, your papa."

"He certainly was."

"We miss him too, Mel. Two beers. Coming up." She turned and disappeared through the café doors.

"You said 'can't dance.' Wish you could. I'd put you to work. You can't believe what I saw today. Ever been to a strip place before?" Mel asked.

"Ever been to a gay bar?"

When they arrived at Mel's home, Johnnie poured himself Chivas Regal neat and joined her on the patio.

"So, how's the arm?" Mel asked.

"Very sore. When I first got shot, it burned like hell. Now it just aches."

"Did they get the bullet?"

"Yeah."

"How'd that work?"

"One of X-Ray's officers, don't remember his name, rode in the ambulance with me. He said to avoid breaking the chain of evidence, the EMT's checked my clothes to make sure the bullet didn't work its way out of my back and get lost en route to the hospital. Then the cop scrubbed and actually came into the operating room for the hand-off, so to speak, of the evidence."

"It was a 9mm."

"I'll take your word on that."

"Haven't found the gun yet. Thank goodness the bullet struck only soft tissue."

He lifted his glass. "Mel, that makes me feel so much better."

Mel slept so hard that when the telephone rang the next morning, her feet tangled in the sheets and she fell on her face on the carpet. The ringing stopped. She scrambled to get disengaged when Rosa called out from the first floor, "Mel. Are you okay? It's

X-Ray. I told him you were sleeping. He says I should wake you and Johnnie. He said it's important."

"I'll get it," she mumbled, and grabbed for the phone. "What the hell you want this time of morning?" Mel picked the clock up as far as the cord would allow and squinted at it.

"I want to invite you to a party we're having."

"I had one last night, thank you very much."

"Sounds like it."

"Where's the party?" Mel asked.

"At the Santa Ana Flood Control Channel on Pacific Coast Highway, between Huntington Beach and Newport Beach."

"What kind of party?"

"It's a game called, 'Identify the Body'."

❖ Chapter 19 ❖

Johnnie, Mel, and X-Ray stood in the parking lot at the end of the Huntington Beach State Park. The Crime Scene Unit of the Orange County Sheriff's Department had yellow POLICE CAUTION—DO NOT CROSS tape strung from the jetty across the end of the parking lot. On the opposite side of the flood waters, the tape ran from a pier under the bridge to the rip-rock line beyond to the ocean entrance. Gulls screeched overhead and shared air space with a small plane pulling a flag banner that read "It's Never Too Late to Find Jesus."

Motorboats idled just off the jetty, while onlookers stared through binoculars.

The click, click, click of bicyclists, in-line skaters, and skateboarders stopped while they, too, gawked at death. Wearing bikinis, tie-dyed shirts, or cut-off jeans, people of all ages, shapes and sizes flocked together at the chance of a gory sighting.

A morbid spectacle. Yet, they can't help themselves. A human needs to see death, Mel thought.

Cars drove across the overpass with a "whomp, whomp" sound that added to the beating the water gave the corpse. The body was trapped against the pilings, amidst the driftwood, broken beer bottles, and plastic rings from beer six-packs. Frothy brown water bubbled around the cadaver, adding to the brew that

103

summed up the fate of yet another human being.

Mel pulled her cap closer on her forehead and peered through dark glasses. "Is it Danko?"

"Could be," X-Ray said. "The coroner will be here any minute, and we'll analyze the prints."

"How'd he die?" Mel asked.

"Looks like gunshot at close range. Small caliber."

"Did he drown before or after being shot?" Johnnie said.

"We won't know 'til the autopsy."

"Where do you think the body fell in the water?" Mel asked.

"It could have been pushed or dropped, Mel," Johnnie replied.

"I don't think so, Johnnie," Mel said. "Buddy was a big guy. It'd take more than one person to overcome him, or lift him, and toss him in. My vote is a fall after being shot."

"Anything's a possibility. Right now, it's hard to tell. The Santa Ana Flood Control Channel covers some seven hundred miles of waterways." X-Ray bent and pointed beyond the barnacled pilings, "And there are some floodgates which close, so the water from the ocean doesn't wash back upstream."

"So, if you get the schedule on openings and closings, you might get a better definition on the time of dumping?" Mel asked.

"I think it must coincide with the tides. I'll check that out, of course."

"Naturally," Mel and Johnnie replied, nodding to each other.

The area signs posted no swimming, no diving, no boating, and no skiing. "Too bad," Mel pointed, "there's no sign that says 'no dying'."

"And no bloating," X-Ray added.

"Your cop humor is lost on me. I'm gonna be sick," Johnnie pivoted; his shoes made grinding sounds in the gravel. He walked near the fence line at the Least Tern Natural Preserve.

Mel and X-Ray chuckled and shook their heads.

"Too much scotch last night?" X-Ray asked.

"Oh, yeah. I never can remember that phrase Lucas uses. Is it whiskey on beer, or beer on whiskey . . . mighty risky? No matter, we started with beer at T.J.'s and Johnnie switched to scotch and me to vodka when we got home."

"Haven't learned yet, huh?" X-Ray smiled a knowing smile.

"God told me I'm still a work in progress."

"Well, his work is finished," X-Ray said, as he pointed to the corpse. "Did Lucas join you in Maui? I forgot to ask."

"No. But he called a lot."

"You're not going to go and get married on me, are you?"

"I'm waiting on you to ask me, X-Ray."

"Well, we're safe there."

An officer from the Orange County Sheriff's Department walked toward Mel and X-Ray and motioned for them to approach the tape. He carried a pad and pen and spoke into a shoulder microphone before addressing them. "The M.E. will be here shortly. Wanna wait?"

"Yeah, we do. We think this is our guy." X-Ray pulled an envelope from his pocket and handed it to the officer. "These are the prints on Danko. We'd like to check 'em against the body."

"You may not have to wait on the M.E. I think the CSI Unit has a fingerprint kit with 'em. Hold on, let me ask." He walked a few paces, pressed the button on the mike near his mouth, and spoke into it. The officer cupped one hand against his earpiece and waited for a response.

It was a deputy Mel had not met before.

No wedding band. Doesn't mean anything, she thought.

"Oh, it's a long, long time, from May to September," she hummed.

Johnnie approached her and wiped his mouth with a tissue. "Mel, for God's sake. We're at a crime scene. Are you flirting?"

"No. A girl can look, can't she?"

"Guys too," Johnnie added, "when they feel good."

"Both of you get a grip," X-Ray said, as he returned to the sandy area where they stood.

"So what's the story?" Mel asked.

"I told the Sheriff's Department that you could probably identify the body. Want to try?"

"Not really. How long's he been there?"

"Bloated like a beached whale."

"Oh, God. You guys are so bad." Johnnie vomited into a paper napkin and ran away from the duo again.

X-Ray and Mel bent under the caution tape and climbed over the rip-rock and driftwood to the shoreline. The distended gray body floated face-up, partially submerged in the water. His eyes bulged through closed lids. The cheeks and lips were swollen and discolored. Long blonde hair swirled about the face, slightly obscuring the earlobes.

Mel watched for a moment, took a deep breath, and said, "Those are the same clothes he had on last night when he broke into the house. The gold earring is fairly generic, but it sure looks like him to me."

"Thank you, Miss . . . ah?"

"Walker. Camellia Walker. My friends call me Mel."

"Any relation to T-Bone Walker, over at Harbour Pointe P.D.?"

106

"My Dad."

"I knew him. Worked a few cases together. Nice man."

"He sure was. Thank you for saying that." Mel smiled at him.

She stepped over small pieces of driftwood and followed X-Ray and the officer away from the crime scene.

Several seagulls made diving runs at the body. The officers scattered them away, then laid a white sheet over Buddy's body.

"Officer, you must know this area pretty well. What can you tell us about time of death? We're just asking for your best guess," X-Ray asked.

"There's a deal here called 'low flow condition' which has something to do with wind-and-wave action. That condition will help the coroner predict the time the body arrived at this point. Water just doesn't come through there all the time. Sometimes it's a lot of water, and sometimes not. When a storm or weather pattern hits the San Bernardino Mountains, the storm breaks through the storage ponds, and all this debris comes out. Sometimes here, or Aliso Creek, or Laguna Beach. Anywhere along those seven hundred miles of flow." The deputy pointed to the channel.

"Could Buddy's body have gone into the water at Back Bay in the San Diego Creek near upper Newport Bay?" Mel asked.

"Yes, he could," the deputy replied. "You have any idea who might have done this?"

She was quick to answer. "No, I don't. Merely seeking information."

"How long before the M.E. arrives?" Johnnie asked.

"CSI can run the latents, if you don't wanna wait for the M.E."

"Whatever you want to do is fine with us." Mel and Johnnie nodded in agreement.

"When did Buddy post bail?" Johnnie asked.

"Yesterday morning, according to the arrest file," X-Ray replied.

"The bail bondsman wouldn't have been Bob Bailey Bonds in Santa Ana by any chance?"

"Lucky guess, Mel?" X-Ray said.

"No. I looked at his federal rap file in L.A. yesterday, and Johnnie checked out the civil and criminal stuff here in Orange County."

"Used Bailey every time," Johnnie answered.

"And I talked with Charlotte, Buddy's girlfriend, yesterday morning," Mel said. "Want us to check with Bailey and find out what Buddy and Charlotte used for collateral?"

"I thought I told you and Johnnie," X-Ray pointed at each one, as he spoke, "not to get involved."

Mel placed both hands on her hips. "Then why did you drag us outta bed at this hour to look at a dead body?"

"Because I wasn't invited to the party last night. Satisfied?"

One Crime Scene Investigator squatted over the sheet-covered body and held one of Buddy's hands. After a few moments, he stood and hollered to the group, "It's Buddy Danko." He waved a card in the air.

"Thank you," X-Ray called back to the analyst.

Mel and Johnnie had quietly backed away and were getting into Mel's car.

X-Ray turned toward them. "Now, where are you two going?"

"Johnnie's sick. I'm going to get him something to drink."

"Stay out of this now. I mean it!" X-Ray shouted.

Mel drove up Brookhurst Street toward Fountain Valley and the freeway. "Why don't we drop by Santa Ana . . . say . . . the area around the courthouse and see if . . ."

"Bob Bailey is working today?" Johnnie finished Mel's sentence.

"What a good idea. I think we will."

"How much more trouble can we get in?"

"What's your best guess?"

"I don't want to know, Mel."

"Notice how you can tell when you're nearing the courthouse?" Mel asked after several moments of silence.

"Yeah. The number of bail bond and law office signs begin to multiply."

"It's easy to see how cops go through burnout. They work their asses off to catch 'em, and these guys bail 'em out before the officer's shift is over."

"Ah, and justice for all. Here we are." Mel bounced over a speed-bump and parked in the shade of a tall eucalyptus tree. The office was an end unit in a small commercial strip. "Look. Stinky still drives that old junker to work."

"That's a front, you know. I see him driving a luxury sedan everywhere else around town. I think he parks this for show."

The glass-front office displayed amateur hand-painted signs, "Fast and Confidential, 24-Hour Service," and *Se Habla Espanol*. A bell chimed somewhere in the rear of the store, as Mel opened the front door.

"Hello Stinky, are you here?" she called out.

"Be right with ya," came a reply from behind a curtain.

A dark-complected man, about six feet tall, packed with two hundred pounds of muscle, limped into the office. His

109

pockmarked face and high cheekbones gave Mel the impression he had Indian blood. He took a long drag on a cigarette and exhaled. The man smiled, displaying his six teeth: two upper and four lower.

"Can I help you?" he asked. "Oh, hi, Mel, Johnnie. What gets you two up and out early this morning?"

"Buddy Danko," Mel answered.

Bailey sat at his oversized desk already cluttered with papers and an overfilled ashtray. "That asshole got me outta bed at two a.m."

"Did he call you direct? Or did his attorney?" Mel asked.

"Asshole called me himself. Collect."

"How'd he know to do that?" Johnnie asked.

"Oh, we advertise in the jail. We have a big sign right near the phone says, 'call collect'."

"Who co-signed the bond, Stinky?" Mel asked.

"The indemnitor? That stripper from the Skin Inn."

"Charlotte?" Mel asked.

"Yeah. That's the one. I think she has a crush on him."

"What'd she put up for the bond?"

"We only take cash, land, houses, or mobile homes."

"No trades, huh?"

"No, Mel. Not like the other guys who swap anything . . . and that includes sex."

"How much was it, if you don't mind our asking?" Johnnie said.

"Let's see." Bob shuffled through the stacks of papers on his desk, then through several green file folders next to a two-tiered in-out basket. "Okay." He pulled one out and opened it. "Home invasion and a felony for possession of a firearm. Let's see," he licked one finger and pulled back two pieces of paper. "That was

$175,000."

"How does that break down?" Mel asked him.

"By statute, the home invasion was one fifty. Then carrying a weapon . . . a felon in possession . . . is another twenty-five. And, Mel, that weapon charge is an automatic five more years in the pen."

"How much real cash did Charlotte have to come up with?"

"Cash, thirteen thousand. Non-refundable like the sign says." Bob pointed to a large white bulletin board with bold red letters in both English and Spanish. "And another thirteen thousand in collateral."

Johnnie looked at Mel. "How'd she come up with that much money at two in the morning?"

"She brought me cold cash for the first part, and I took the title to her mobile home that's free and clear for the collateral." Bob crushed the cigarette butt into the ashtray. He coughed up phlegm, picked up a gray trash can and spit into it. Then he pulled a fresh cigarette from his pocket and lit it up.

"Does she get the 'pink slip' to her home back?" Mel asked.

"Yep. When Buddy shows up in court for all his appearances and gets his final sentencing. Then the bond is exonerated and I give her the title."

"Does Buddy have an attorney?"

"I haven't heard from one yet."

"So you're the babysitter."

"Yeah. Charlotte and me. Our job is to see he makes all appearances."

"What if he doesn't get to court? Maybe isn't able to for some reason?" Mel asked.

"I'll find him and kill him," Bob replied.

"Somebody already beat you to it."

111

❖ Chapter 20 ❖

Mel drove Johnnie to their office where several telephone messages awaited them.

"Hi, you two. This is X-Ray. Where are you? I told you not to get involved. You better not be working on the Danko case. I'm at the office."

"Call home, please," was Rosa's message.

"Mel, this is Sam from the Skin Inn. Call me."

"Who do we call first?" Johnnie asked.

"You call Rosa. Scat probably came home. I'll take the other two."

"Okay. Then I have a few appointments this afternoon I need to make."

"New case?"

"Yeah. One's a weenie waggler and the other's a car jacking."

"A pedophile?"

"I don't think so. Just some guy who likes to show everyone his privates."

"Dangerous?"

"No attacks or overtures yet. But he does hang around middle schools exposing himself to young girls."

"That's just too sick."

"You know what we call that, don't you?"

"Yeah. Job security," Mel said.

"I'll catch up with you later." Johnnie kissed Mel on the cheek and left.

Mel's printer whirred away for several minutes filling the bin with paper.

Hmm. Charlotte has no police record in Orange or L.A. County. I wonder if that's unusual for an exotic dancer. No prostitution. No solicitation. Never married. No kids. Owns the mobile home free and clear. Bought it before the robbery. Made usual payments. No big bank or saving accounts. Lives alone ... unless Buddy threw his clothes there.

The phone rang.

"Why didn't you call me back?"

"Hi, X-Ray. Johnnie and I just got back, and you were my next call. What's happening?"

"Several things. Well, now we know that Buddy Danko was killed with a 9mm."

"Same gun that killed Peter?"

"We don't have the ballistics back yet."

"Well, last night I accused Buddy of killing Peter, and he vehemently denied it. Buddy had no real reason to lie because he was holding the gun on us."

"So you think he really was looking for the bank money?"

"That's what he said. He said he thought Peter had given me the money and he wanted his share. That's all."

"There's another thing."

"Yeah."

"The safety deposit key you gave me that you took from Peter's home?"

"Right."

"The money isn't there either. We got a court order and pulled the box this morning after you and Johnnie left the crime scene."

"How do you know which bank it belonged to?"

"Key is coded. We get the location of the actual branch from the banking . . . say, I don't need to tell you everything I know."

"Anything important in there? Any trail?" Mel asked.

"None that I'm going to share with you. You're not working on this, remember? Now, Mel, two people have been murdered, maybe by the same person who is still out there, and knows you're involved in this case. See where I'm going on this?"

"Don't worry about Johnnie or me."

"Watch your back. If something ever happened to you, I'd never forgive you."

"We'll be fine, X. I have some files to work on. Remember, I just got back from vacation. I've got a new fraud case. By the way, have you notified Peter's mother?" Mel asked.

"Yes, we did."

"Took it hard, huh?"

"Very. She had a small life insurance policy on him and is planning his funeral using those funds."

"So, she isn't swimming in big bucks either. That rules her out."

"Not unless she's lying to me and I don't think she is. Lady lives a very meager existence. And Mel?"

"Yeah?"

"Don't bother her. I've already questioned her. She has no idea why he changed his name to Paul Cooper. A very nice, sweet lady who had only one child. She adored Peter and his family and now they're gone. She's going to have a rough time without more questions from you. Promise?"

"I promise that."

"Fine. Talk with you later."

"Bye," she said.

Follow the money. Where is the money? Mel thought as she hung up the phone receiver.

She placed another call. "Hi, this is Mel Walker. Is Sam in? He called me." Classical music filled the background as she waited.

"Hi, Mel."

"Sam. You called?"

"Yeah. Why didn't you tell us Buddy was murdered when you were here yesterday?"

"Well, first of all that isn't my job . . . telling anybody. That's for the police to do. Second, I didn't know Buddy was killed until the police called me this morning and told me."

"Why didn't you tell us Peter was dead?"

"Sam, like I said, that's the responsibility of the police department . . . notifying family and all. I get in enough trouble without aggravating the police."

"Charlotte is crying her eyes out. She loved Buddy, you know?"

"Thought you both had kind of a crush on her."

"We did and I still do. She's so beautiful and sweet. Do just about anything for anybody. Wonderful dancer and so kind. You'll never know."

Mel tested the waters. "I'll be honest with you, Sam. I'm on the trail of the money from the bank robbery. Peter hired me to find it before he was murdered."

115

"What? He didn't have it? We always thought Peter double-crossed Buddy."

"I thought so too. But Buddy broke into my house the other night and told me he never saw it after he was arrested. He thought Peter gave it to me when he hired me."

"Well, where is it then?"

"Sam, that's a damn good question."

❖ Chapter 21 ❖

Peter Connelly's obituary notice appeared in the *Harbour Pointe News* the following morning.

> Funeral services will be held today at 10 a.m. at the Harbour View Memorial Park for long time resident, Peter Connelly age 57. Mr. Connelly is survived by his mother Naomi. His wife Darlene, and daughter Stacy preceded him in death. He previously worked for the Western Guaranty Bank in Los Angeles. Gravesite services will be private. At the family's request, in lieu of flowers, donations should be made to Mothers Against Drunk Drivers.

Mel emptied her tea cup, wiped her mouth, and stood. Cool breezes blew from the Pacific across her backyard and patio. She yawned and stretched her arms, welcoming the wind.

"Good morning," Johnnie said. He pushed the newly fixed slider open and walked to the dining table.

"What's so good about it?"

"My, aren't we testy this morning."

"I don't do mornings."

"What's the alternative?"

"Smart-ass." Mel leaned forward and kissed Johnnie on the cheek. He returned the affection. "How's your arm feeling? You haven't complained."

"It's doing much better. I have a doctor's appointment today and I should be able to start exercising it soon. I sure don't want that arm to freeze up. That's just what I need . . . arthritis."

"Want me to run you over there?"

"No. I'll be fine. But thanks for the offer."

"Time for your bath?" Rosa called out from inside the slider door.

"No," Johnnie replied. "I'll be fine. I can do it myself. Thank you, though."

"Coward," Mel whispered.

"Got a yellow stripe the size of Montana down my back."

"So, beside seeing Doc Townsend, what's on tap for today?"

"Need to canvas a couple of my 'weenie waggler's' neighbors."

"Looking for a pattern of behavior?"

"Yeah. What are you up to?"

"First, I'm going to a funeral."

"Peter's or Buddy's?"

"Peter's. After that . . . can you keep a secret?"

"Sure." Johnnie moved near Mel and lowered his head.

"Me, too," Rosa said, as she opened the glass door, stepped onto the patio, and set a fresh plate of sliced fruit on the table. "I can keep a secret."

"I'm going to see a plastic surgeon today." Mel pulled the skin on her face up with one finger and the loose skin under the neck with her thumb. "What do you think?"

Johnnie and Rosa laughed. Johnnie coughed and Rosa spat

saliva.

"You should see yourself," Johnnie said.

She dropped her hands and smiled weakly. "Bummer. Too severe, huh?"

"You look like a skin on a drum," Johnnie said.

Mel pointed to the sides of her face. "Maybe just a little chemical peel to remove these wrinkles. What do you think, Rosa?"

"Rosa thinks you look *muy bonita* just the way you are. And your dad and mom would say that too."

"That's a good idea, I'll stop by and talk with Mom, Dad, and Willie about it. See you later tonight."

"Don't do anything without talking with us first. Promise?"

"I won't. Today's appointment is just a consultation."

Rosa giggled as she snapped up a dirty dish. "Sound's like she's going to the body shop, Johnnie, and getting a repair estimate."

The fragrant and colorful blooms of winter greeted Mel as she drove through the stucco columned entrance of Harbour View Memorial Park. She followed the winding road to the back near a large stand of eucalyptus and cypress trees, their leaves blowing a frantic call in the winter wind. She parked the car, removed a rag and a can from the trunk, and walked to the family gravesite. She finishing polishing the headstones, then sat cross-legged on the grass.

"Okay family, I found my first gray hair. We have to talk."

Mel stood and walked to the funeral service several hundred feet away. The wind velocity increased and leaves, sticks, and flower petals swirled around her. She counted seven mourners. Boards were placed across the open ground, a steel gray casket lay on top of them, and the mound of dirt opposite the site was covered by a green velvet tarp. A small tent had been erected, and five folding chairs faced the coffin. An elderly white-haired woman gripped a torn tissue and wept. Charlotte and Sam stood in the small gathering. Mel joined them as the sermon began.

"Father, we are gathered here to remember your son, Peter Connelly. We thank you for the brief time we had to know and love this fine son, father, husband, and friend. His tragic death leaves us to wonder why someone would violate such an important commandment. Help this close circle of friends and family to understand and accept Peter's fate. For Peter Connelly is now free to spend eternity with his beloved Darlene and Stacy. Go in peace. Amen."

The black-robed minister walked to the elderly woman and whispered something to her. She wept and dabbed her eyes beneath the dark glasses. The man shook each person's hand, as he walked around the tented area, then put sunglasses on, and turned toward the mortuary.

Mel nodded to Sam and Charlotte, approached the woman and extended her hand. "Mrs. Connelly? I'm Mel Walker, a friend of your son. I'm sorry for your loss."

Naomi Connelly shielded her eyes with one hand and extended the other. "Thank you, Miss, uh Walker, is it?"

"Yes. I've only known him a brief time. But he was a fine man."

"Thank you, dear."

"I know this probably isn't a good time to ask you, but . . ."

"Honey, if he owed you money, I can't help you. I barely had enough funds from the insurance policy to bury him."

"Oh, it isn't money. I'd like for you to look around and tell me if you know everybody here."

"Looking for someone special?"

"Just trying to find something out, Mrs. Connelly."

Mel backed away. Four other people, three men and one woman, shook Naomi's hand and, in hushed voices, offered their condolences. Mel picked up some dirt and sprinkled it on the casket, adding her "may you rest in peace" thoughts.

She felt a tap on her back and turned.

"Charlotte and I are glad you came today, Mel. We wanted you to know," Sam said.

"I felt I should be here. I guess he didn't have many friends."

"Not any, really," Charlotte said. "The bank folks never forgave him the robbery, and he wasn't like the ex-cons he spent time in prison with. He was kinda in limbo, between two worlds. One that he couldn't have, and one that he didn't want."

It was the first time Mel realized how baby-like Charlotte's voice sounded. Soft, infantile, and weepy, like a cartoon character.

Sam looked at Mel and at Charlotte and asked, "She cleans up right pretty, don't she, Mel?"

"I was just thinking, you do look lovely today, Charlotte. And you must be right about that. How very sad for him, for all of you."

Charlotte sighed and stepped backwards as Naomi neared.

"Miss Walker," Naomi Connelly said.

"Yes."

"About your question?"

"Yes, ma'am."

"I know everyone. You know Sam and Charlotte already." She turned to the others still near the coffin. "And these are neighbors of mine and his landlord."

"I felt I should ask. Thank you."

Naomi held Mel's arm in a death grip. "Are you gonna help me find out who murdered my boy?"

"Well, I . . ."

"I knew God would send somebody to help me."

"Really . . . no. A few days ago Peter asked me to do some work for him. I merely felt I should try to finish my assignment before I close my file."

Naomi gripped Mel's shirt, pulled Mel down to her height and whispered in her ear, "You're looking for the money?"

Mel nodded.

"When you find the money, you'll find the murderer. God bless."

❖ Chapter 22 ❖

Mel walked across the graveled path toward her car and jingled the keys. The noise of wheels skidding on the small pebbles drew her attention toward a black sedan that careened through the exit and disappeared from view. She approached the Mercedes and noticed a small piece of white paper fluttering under the windshield wipers. The typed unsigned message was clear: "Stay out of this. It isn't any of your business. You will get hurt."

A blonde, middle-aged woman approached Mel. She carried a clipboard and pen.

"If you'll fill out these 'new patient' forms, please. I'll be right with you."

Mel completed the paperwork, then stared at the colorful angel fish swimming from one end of the aquarium to the other when a voice startled her. "Miss Walker?"

"Yes." She stood and followed the nurse down the hallway to a small examination room.

"Have a seat." The nurse directed Mel to an armchair covered in zebra-printed fabric. "I'll check your vitals and Dr. Reynolds will be in to talk with you."

Mel pushed up the sleeve on her white shirt and the nurse wrapped the blood pressure cuff around her arm. She sucked on a flat strip of the sharp-edged plastic thermometer as her eyes wandered to the picture frames on the wall. Dr. Reynolds had quite a collection of diplomas.

Mel squinted to check the dates of completion on one diploma, when the nurse pulled the vinyl tab from her mouth. The sharp edges stung. Cold fingers reached for her wrist to feel the pulse rate. Mel didn't feel particularly chatty and neither did the nurse. The woman made a few notes on Mel's chart and took it with her when she left the room.

She picked up a fashion magazine, and thumbed through a few pages before Dr. Reynolds came in.

"Hello, Miss Walker. Glad you came to see me."

The doctor's hairdresser must work overtime to get that great shade of red, Mel thought.

"Hello, Dr. Reynolds. Please call me Mel."

"You're so gracious. Let's see." The doctor scanned the chart and sat on a small swivel stool near the sink.

The doctor wore a three-quarter length, white smock, black linen pants, and black pumps. Her nails were neatly manicured. The watch appeared to be gold and so did the necklace she had worn on Mel's earlier visit. But it was a plain gold band on the third finger of the left hand that caught Mel's eye.

Striking woman, Mel thought. Neat, strong and beautiful.

"Why don't you sit up here and let's take a look at your skin."

"I'm here, you know, for a consultation. I'm not sure I want or need anything done."

"Mel, all women say that when they come to see me. Afterwards, they all say, 'I'll never do that surgery again.' They all

124

do."

Mel chuckled as she climbed onto the examining table. Dr. Reynolds took an instrument that resembled a large magnifying glass with a light and scanned back and forth across Mel's face.

"Close your eyes, please. The light can be a bit bright."

With her eyes closed, Mel smelled an aroma from Dr. Reynolds which brought back memories of her grandmother.

"Hmm. You have a lot of deep skin damage. When you get older, more freckles and skin discolorations will give you problems. You should make some corrections now."

"Like what, for instance?"

"First, I would suggest a chemical peel."

"That sounds dangerous. Like acid rain."

Dr. Reynolds smiled, "No, actually the procedure can be done under a local anesthetic, right here in our offices. I apply the solution to your face. It causes the top layer to become red as it heals, but it's very good for minor wrinkles and crow's-feet."

"How many days would I be unable to work or be seen in public?"

"While it's healing, I can recommend some wonderful makeup that covers the redness, so you can continue to work. I have one feisty patient who had a complete facelift, including a chemical peel, and went to Las Vegas eleven days after surgery."

"Wow."

"Why don't you sit up for me? Let's take a good look at gravity."

Dr. Reynolds pulled and tugged Mel's chin and the area around her ears and forehead.

"I'm getting a turkey neck, aren't I?" she asked.

"Pretty close. You know, it's never too early to challenge Father Time. And while you are a beauty, Mel, I think a chemical peel would be an appropriate way to begin. Then when that heals, we can look at a full lift sometime within . . . oh say . . . the next year or so."

"What's the chemical peel cost?"

"Let me have my consultant come in and talk with you. Remember insurance doesn't cover this type of work. But we'll work a payment schedule for you, if full payment can't be made at one time."

"I'll talk about the chemical peel. But, I'm not ready to go under-the-knife without thinking about it a while."

"Chicken?"

"Gobble. Gobble. Gobble," Mel smiled.

Talking with a high-powered salesperson for twenty minutes convinced Mel that the woman's salary depended entirely on commissions. She politely told the consultant she wanted to discuss the chemical peel with her family before making a final commitment or scheduling the procedure. Mel left Dr. Reynolds' office and drove to her own.

She entered Dr. Sarah Reynolds' name in several search engines on the Internet and waited.

Hmm. The good doctor does a land-office business in surgery. No malpractice cases on file according to records in Sacramento. Although she might have settled them before the lawsuits were filed. That would have kept them off the state records. Probably has a large deductible. Graduate of Stanford, been a surgeon for more than ten years. No pending or closed litigation of any nature, civil or criminal. That's good news, Mel thought.

Dr. Reynolds' website contained glowing reports from "satisfied customers" who signed themselves "Joan F." and "Kathy B."

The real estate records appeared on screen. The good doctor owns the building where her offices are. And a nice list of other property holdings. Going to have to look at those.

For no particular reason Mel ran DMV, hit the Print button, and called the Harbour Pointe Police Department.

"Hi, this is Mel. Is X-Ray in?"

"No, he isn't. Want to leave a message for him?" the flat voice she did not recognize replied.

"I'm returning his call. Ask him to track me down. I need to talk with him too."

"Sure thing."

Her next call was to Barry Zabel.

"Orange County Coroner's Office."

"Hi, Sally. This is Mel."

"How are you?"

"Fine. Is Barry in?"

"Full house today. He's here, but dictating and cutting. Can I have him call you back?"

"Sure. I'm at the office for a while yet. I'll be home later."

"Great. I'll have him call."

"Sounds good. Bye." Mel hung up and returned to her computer.

Dr. Reynolds owns a new SL500 Mercedes, a Porsche Carrera, and a Silver Shadow Rolls Royce. An automobile for every occasion, Mel thought.

Doc's a Republican, but then so is most of Orange County. Her listed age, ouch, forty-seven, single and no evidence of children. I wouldn't have guessed her to be that old. Her face is so perfect. I wonder who did "her" facelift?

The phone rang, disrupting Mel's thoughts.

"Walker Investigations. May I help you?"

"Returning your call, Mel. What's happening?"

"Hi, Barry. I have a few questions for you. Do you have time to see me?"

"Not today. We're playing to a full house. They're stacked two-deep in the hallway."

"A massacre?"

"Full moon, more likely."

"How about if I drop by tomorrow afternoon, late?"

"That's better. I should have many of the cadavers processed by then. Most are gunshot and stabbing victims anyway."

"See you then."

The Skin Inn was next on Mel's phone list.

"Hi, there."

"Hi, back. This is Mel Walker. Is Sam there today?"

"Sure. Sam," she hollered, "phone call."

Applause died down, and the disc jockey called for the next dancer. "Let's put your hands together for Darlene from Queens. Come on up, Darlene, and let's entertain our troops at home."

Mel heard a drum roll, then a man's voice.

"Hi, Mel."

"Hello, Sam. Can I ask you a favor?"

"Sure. Mrs. Connelly told us you were helping her."

"I need your last name, social security number, and date of birth."

"Wha . . .?" Sam's voice reflected his surprise.

"I'm following the money trail. I need that information on both you and Charlotte, so I research and eliminate you as suspects. Any problem with that?"

128

"Ah . . . I guess not. 'Cause Charlotte and me, we're poor as church mice. My bar tab here is over a hundred bucks and I don't get my social security check for two more weeks. I got nothin' to hide."

"And Charlotte?"

"Her, neither. Would she be takin' her clothes off if she had a quarter million bucks stashed somewhere?"

"I agree that makes sense, but I'd be doing a lousy job of investigating if I didn't check out all involved parties."

"It's Smith and Kerns."

"What is?"

"Our last names. Mine is Smith. Hers Kerns."

Mel ran every asset program she had on Sam, no middle name, Smith and Charlotte Jean Kerns. Sam still rented an apartment. Charlotte's mobile home, once free and clear, now had a lien from Bob Bailey Bonds. Both paid notes on older model sedans, were single, did not vote, had no kids or bank accounts. Charlotte had an enormous balance on a debt-consolidation loan, paying thirteen and one-half percent interest.

Ouch, Mel thought, counting her blessings.

The phone rang.

"Walker Investigations. Mel Walker speaking."

"X here. Busy?"

"No, not really. I was returning your call."

"Wanted you to know we made a clean sweep of Peter Connelly aka Paul Cooper's home."

"And . . .?"

"Nothing. We found nothing. No leads as to the money or the killer."

"Too bad."

"Did you take anything except the safety deposit key you gave me?"

"No. Why?"

"He had a small savings account. Found that passbook. But only a couple of grand in it."

"Any correspondence with family or friends?"

"Except for monthly bills, not even a Christmas card."

"Tough," Mel said.

"About the bullets?"

"Yeah?"

"The same 9mm used to shoot Johnnie killed both Peter and Buddy. Ballistics back this morning. The land and grooves from all three shells match."

"So, in all likelihood, Buddy may not have killed Peter and may not have shot Johnnie."

"I suspect Buddy did shoot them, and then someone turned the gun on Buddy."

"Why is that? Wasn't the gun you took away from Buddy at my house the same one used in all of the shootings?"

"No, as a matter of fact, it wasn't. We still have that weapon in the evidence room. We found the 9mm in Buddy's car."

"Which was parked where?"

"The Orange County Sheriff's Department found the car resting on the bottom of Irvine Lake," X-Ray replied.

"With the gun?"

"In the trunk."

"Like someone drove his car there and abandoned it?"

"Hoping that it'd never be recovered in the muddy bottom."

"Any latents on the gun or DNA in the car?"

"Working on that right now. Listen. Despite my orders, I know you, Mel. You're working this on your faithful computer. Things it'd take me weeks or months to develop. Kick out with it. What do you have so far?"

"Dead end here too. I ran his mother, Naomi Connelly, and Sam Smith and Charlotte Kerns from the Skin Inn. All living a marginal existence. Honestly, I don't know how some people make it in this world."

"Me either, Mel. We're very lucky."

"Dad leaving me some extra money made my life easier. But I'd give it all back to have him here with me."

"I know."

"I'm doing some good things with the extra funds."

"What?"

"Going to get involved in some charity work. Rosa helps with a battered woman's shelter. I think Mom and Dad would approve."

"Absolutely. I'm really proud of you, lady. And I love you a lot."

"Me too, X."

"So, Mel. I need you to do one additional thing for me in your searches."

"What's that?"

"Show me the money."

❖ Chapter 23 ❖

Mel worked well past lunch the next day on a fraud case. She had interviewed several witnesses, taken three handwritten statements under penalty of perjury, and dictated a report to the attorney.

She arrived at the Coroner's Office located on the large campus of buildings that made up the Orange County government system. Mel brushed her hair, applied fresh lipstick, and popped a couple of breath mints in her mouth before exiting the car.

The slate-gray, paneled walls and glossy tiled floors always appeared to match what lay behind the reception doors: a grim, gray reminder of nameless, faceless bodies who would be cleansed by clergy and God. A human's last opportunity to be acknowledged for his or her contribution in this life. Mel shivered. She had been here more often than most mortals.

"Afternoon, Sally."

"Hi, Mel. Go on in. Barry's got more bodies than brains, but he's expecting you."

Mel waited on the security buzzer, slipped a visitor's badge on her white collar, and pushed the steel doors.

The wide hallway, well lit with the eerie glow of fluorescent and permeated with the strong smell of anesthetic, greeted her.

132

Several double-wide doors lined the walkway. Mel stood on tiptoes and peeked in each door as she passed. Autopsies were being performed by extra medical examiners, some of them on contract to the county. At the last door, Mel looked in, then knocked.

"Come in," was the directive. She took a deep breath and pushed the door open.

"Take some Vaseline if you like."

"Will I need it? I've done this before."

"I did. This one's ripe. Been cooking a couple of days."

Mel walked to a shiny, steel counter top covered with vials, slides, and microscopes. She saw a jar of the odorless, gray-green goo, dabbed two fingers in the jar, then smeared it under her nose and wiped her fingers on a tissue. She turned to face Barry, but kept her eyes from looking directly at the corpse, whose organs were exposed from breastbone to pubis.

"What'd you need to see me about today?"

"Barry, I swear you get better looking every time I see you."

"Flattery? You came all the way to tell me I'm a stud-muffin?"

"No. I need a little advice, guidance, if you will."

"Shoot."

"What if you were losing your looks?"

"Are you now saying I'm getting old?" He switched the saw off and held it at an angle pointed to the sky.

"Naw. Just play along with me. Would you, you know . . ." She patted the underside of her chin with the back of her fingers, "get some work done?"

"I probably wouldn't. But I've got Beth and six kids to house, feed, and educate."

"How about me? Would you recommend I do something?"

"When?"

133

"Now."

"What?"

Mel straddled a chrome stool across the table from the cadaver. She turned her head away and took another deep breath through her mouth.

"A chemical peel."

Barry laid the saw on an equipment tray and picked up a bloody scalpel. He pointed to the edge of his face near the temple. Blood dripped from his wet glove. "You mean here, your crow's-feet?"

Mel jumped up and that set the stool in a spin. "See. You agree I have wrinkles."

He waved the gleaming instrument at her. "I didn't say that. I was merely suggesting that's where most men and women generally start their wrinkling."

"Is surgery dangerous?"

"Anytime you undergo anesthesia of any kind you're at risk, Mel. And although I've never done it, seen it done, nor know anyone personally who had plastic surgery . . . all surgery is a risk."

Mel pointed at the body. "Ever know anyone to die during or after surgery?"

"Strange you should ask that."

"Why?"

"I got one in deep freeze. Just came in this morning."

❖ Chapter 24 ❖

"Male or female?" Mel asked.

"Male. Body-builder type. Mid thirties. Good-looking guy."

"Did he die because of the plastic surgery?"

"After a pec lift in the recovery room. Heart attack probably. All those guys take anabolic steroids and, to some degree, suffer heart stress for the rest of their lives."

"What's a pec lift?"

Barry snapped the rubber gloves off, tossed them and a mask into a cloth-lined trash bin as he directed Mel to the holding room. He touched his breast area and made an uplifting gesture under them.

"Medically it's called *gynecomstia,* a Greek word for 'woman-like breasts.' It's much more common in men than most people think. An estimated forty to sixty percent of men, especially those over the age of fifty, have this condition. Of course, you can develop them in other ways, including drug and alcohol use.

"But I think this guy is someone who worked out . . . played sports . . . whatever, to get buff. Once they've started exercising, they have to keep it up forever, so to speak. When they don't, their tits begin to sag like everyone else. Gravity kicks in."

"Do you know how the surgery is performed?"

"Sure. The procedure is to go in here." He pointed in an

arcing wave. "Make an incision. Remove the fatty tissue by liposuction, and tighten the muscles. This is usually done around the areola of the nipple. Gives a guy tight tits."

"Jeez. That sounds painful," Mel shuddered.

"It was . . . for him. Cost him his life."

"Who was his attending physician?"

"A Dr. Adams, I believe. Not someone I know."

"Me either. Why are you doing an autopsy? I didn't think one was necessary in California when the patient is attended by a doctor?"

"Ex-wife had him sent over here. She thought he was much too healthy to die this way. Asked us to look into it for her."

"Could the deceased be anyone I know?"

"Take a look for yourself."

Barry and Mel entered a small mausoleum. The walls were lined with life-size filing cabinets. He picked up a chart, studied it a moment, then walked to a steel door marked number three and yanked the drawer open.

❖ Chapter 25 ❖

Mel drank her vodka and tonic and stared at the pink horizon as the last vestiges of sun kissed the horizon on its way to Hawaii. A voice interrupted her daydreaming.

"So, who was it?" Johnnie asked.

"No one I knew. Thank God."

"What did the surgery look like?"

"You are so morbid. Honestly, I couldn't get past that handsome face. That sad, cold, pasty-gray face." She gulped down her drink.

Johnnie poured himself another Chivas Regal, reached into the ice bucket and plopped some ice cubes into his cocktail glass.

"We never get used to seeing dead people do we?" he said.

"I never have."

"How many have you seen?"

"Jesus, Johnnie, that's not something you count."

Both Johnnie and Mel sat mesmerized by the shocking pink-to-orange dot dropping behind the horizon.

"So, where are we on this damn case . . . ground zero? I don't have a clue. What are we missing here?"

"We must not be overlooking too much. Otherwise why did I get a warning today?"

"What warning?"

"At the cemetery. Someone left me an epistle suggesting that I mind my own business."

"Do you have the note? Let me see it."

"I tossed it. Nobody, nothing is going to scare us off this case."

Johnnie jumped up and ran into the house. When he returned a few minutes later, he carried two pencils, a big eraser, and a roll of butcher paper he spread open across the tabletop.

"If it helps the police department story-board their cases, it'll damn well work for us," Johnnie said.

The night wind gusted, so Johnnie and Mel placed the bottle of Chivas Regal at one corner of the paper and a half-empty bottle of vodka in the other. Each took a pencil and began to draw and label circles with conjoining lines, like atoms and their nuclei.

"Okay. Peter Connelly, a.k.a. Paul Cooper, mild-mannered bank teller, had a terrible run of bad luck. He met . . ."

"Here's Buddy Danko, star of bars and bodies."

"They're loners. They meet, plan, and execute a bank robbery."

"They agree on a hiding place, but Peter takes the loot."

"Buddy gets the shaft."

"Each goes to prison."

"Peter first. Then Buddy. Peter might have had time to move the loot from the agreed place," Mel added.

"Assuming they did discuss that point. I don't believe either of them was too bright."

"No argument there. Then Peter paroles first. The money is gone."

"Did Buddy have a chance to move it?"

"No. He entered prison last and got out last. Peter is the only person who had possession and opportunity to move it."

"Okay. Then a male murders Peter."

"Who might or might not have been Buddy," Mel said.

"And shoots me."

"Yeah."

"Buddy? Are we sure Buddy shot Peter or me?"

"He told us he didn't."

"What if he lied?"

"Then Buddy gets murdered by . . .?"

"There's another dead-end."

"Neither Naomi, Peter's mother, nor Sam and Charlotte from the Skin Inn, shows any evidence of having the motive, opportunity, or the means to pull this off."

"Except . . ." Mel sat in the chair and bit down on her pencil.

"Except what?"

"I ran assets on Charlotte. No exciting bank transactions. She owned her mobile home. But that's now mortgaged thanks to Buddy's bail-bondsman. She has car notes and a debt consolidation loan." Mel stared at Johnnie. "Where the hell did she get the thirteen thousand dollars . . . in cash, to bail Buddy out of jail at two o'clock in the morning, the day after he broke in here . . ."

Johnnie finished Mel's sentence, ". . .so he could be killed."

The pain behind Mel's eyes intensified, as she became conscious of her surroundings. The white, blinding sun came through the wooden slats of the bedroom shutters at the exact minute Mel heard a phone ring in the deep recesses of her brain. She rolled over and heard X-Ray's voice on the recorder.

"Mel, are you there? Pick up."

She groped for the receiver, dropped it once and mumbled, "No need to holler. I can hear you fine."

X-Ray whispered, "Oh, is your little head hurting again this morning?"

"Shut up," she snarled back.

"Oh, and we're in a really, really, bad mood, too?"

Silence.

Mel laid the receiver on the pillow and gently lowered her head beside it.

"Mel. Mel? Listen to me."

"What do you want for God's sake? What time is it?" Mel fumbled for the clock.

"It's not that early. I have some news for you. Are you listening?"

"Shoot, softly," Mel whispered.

"I have a suspect on the Connelly and Danko murders."

❖ Chapter 26 ❖

Mel let the warm water wash over her head and hair in a steady stream. She dried, then dressed in jeans and a denim shirt, and popped a tattered Houston Oiler cap over her damp hair. The smell of onions cooking wafted upstairs, nauseating her. She gagged, swallowed a couple of aspirins with water from her toothpaste rinse-glass and walked toward the eye-tearing odor.

"Who's cooking in my kitchen?"

"Good morning sleepyhead," Johnnie said, his voice starting at a higher octave than usual. He stirred something in the skillet and added, "Breakfast's ready."

"I don't know if I can look at eggs this early in the morning."

"Sure you can. Plus a little 'hair-of-the-dog' as they say in the drinking business."

Mel picked up a tiny bottle with red liquid in it and squinted at the label, "What's this?"

"Dog hair. Smell it. It'll clear up your head."

"Wow," she turned her head away from the open jar, "Tabasco Sauce."

"Just what the puppy ordered." Johnnie carried a plate to the breakfast room table and set it down in front of Mel. "*Mangia. Mangia.*"

"I'm not sure my stomach wants to eat."

Johnnie laid his plate down across the table from Mel and picked up his fork. "Who was that on the phone?"

"X. He wants us there right after breakfast." She paused, looked at her eggs, then at Johnnie. "He's arrested a suspect."

"Interesting. On what case?"

"Ours, of course."

Johnnie choked on his mouthful of eggs, drank from a glass of milk, and asked, "Who is it?"

"He didn't . . . or rather wouldn't . . . tell me."

"Then, why the hell would he want us down there?"

"The suspect asked for us by name."

Johnnie and Mel entered the reception room and waved at the civil service employee whose name escaped Mel's foggy mind. Today she called him Mack. He glanced at them for an instant and the door clicked open. She and Johnnie crossed the almost empty squad room. Several uniformed officers nodded and smiled. Mel had known most of them since her father first brought her to the department when she was old enough to walk. Whitey, one of the undercover cops, approached Mel and hugged her.

"Don't you look nice and smell good too?" she said.

Whitey touched his shoulder-length, white hair. "Had it trimmed up a bit."

"And a suit yet. Get a promotion or something?" Johnnie asked.

"Naw. This is my 'going to court' suit. I must admit taking a warm bath and putting on cologne is something I don't do often enough. I like it."

"Me too. Last time I saw you, you had a more . . ."

"A man-of-the-street odor?" Johnnie offered.

The trio laughed. Mel inhaled the scent of fresh coffee and donuts. "That's a familiar odor. Now I can eat," she said.

They moved to the kitchenette on one side of the room. Mel picked up a mug and filled it. She took a maple bar and turned. "Where's Dad's desk?"

The squad room's desks, chairs, and credenzas had been rearranged into rows on each side of a wide walkway. The institution-style desks were gray and cream-colored metal. Her eyes considered each as she passed on the way to Chief Murdoch's office.

X-Ray greeted her and Johnnie with a nod and one finger motioning them to "come in." They entered Chief Murdoch's office and X-Ray closed the door behind them. The chief stood, hugged Mel, and shook Johnnie's hand.

"You look thinner than I've seen you in a while. On a diet?" Mel asked.

"Yeah, Margaret's got me some special deal. Eating lots of raw vegetables."

"And," X-Ray added, "when he can get away from her, he scarfs down donuts."

Everyone chuckled, which set the tone for Mel's next question.

"Where's Dad's desk?"

"Mel, honey, after the holidays, we decided to redo the office. His wooden desk didn't fit the new, you know, official government look. And well, we thought you might like to have it. It's in storage. When you can get a minute, we'll move it to your office for you."

143

"I'd like that."

The chief looked at Johnnie. "How's the arm doing? I see you got your sling off."

Johnnie rotated the right arm and winced. "It's going to be in the low seventies today."

They all laughed again.

"Got one of those temperature gauges myself, Johnnie. I know the feeling." Chief Murdoch rubbed the right side of his clavicle. "So, you're both wondering why I called this meeting?"

"Yeah. Who is this mysterious suspect?" Mel asked.

"And why would you want us here?" Johnnie asked.

"The suspect asked for you. Said they didn't kill anyone. Wants to hire you two to prove their innocence," X-Ray said.

"Who is it?" Mel asked.

"Your friend, Terry," X-Ray replied.

Mel and Johnnie looked at each other and in unison said, "Terry who?"

❖ Chapter 27 ❖

Mel, Johnnie, X-Ray, and Chief Murdoch stood in the small alcove next to the interrogation room and peered through the one-way mirror that covered most of one wall.

Johnnie spoke first. "Who the hell is Terry?"

Mel pointed at the sad-eyed woman wearing a crocheted bra who slouched deep in the wooden chair and fiercely puffed on a cigarette. "That's the bartender from the Skin Inn."

"She may be the bartender, but she's also the owner," X-Ray said.

Mel turned to X-Ray. "No. That can't be right. I went in there and asked for Terry, the owner. This woman," she pointed at the mirror, "told me HE was out."

"I'd lie too, if you came barging into my place of business, asking a lot of questions," Chief Murdoch said.

"And you think she killed Buddy?" Mel asked.

"We've got a pretty solid case against her," X-Ray volunteered.

"You think Buddy shot Peter and Johnnie. Then Terry killed Buddy?" Mel asked.

"And we've got a great trail on the money too," Chief Murdoch said.

"Did she confess?" Johnnie asked.

Chief Murdoch scratched his thinning gray hair, glanced up at the ceiling, and replied, "Not exactly."

"And you've got the money in your hot little hands?" Johnnie asked.

"Not exactly," X-Ray said.

"Now," Mel nodded, "the picture is getting clearer. You want Johnnie and me to get 'em both?"

"Exactly," Chief Murdoch smiled and rubbed his belly.

"Why would she tell me anything she wouldn't tell you?" Mel asked.

"Ask her yourself." X-Ray walked to the door and put his hand on the knob.

"Oh, this is really clear now. She's lawyered up, isn't she?"

Both cops looked at the suspect through the window without responding.

"And her attorney is . . .?" Johnnie asked.

At that moment, the door of the interrogation room opened and a well-dressed man entered the room, walked over to the window, and pulled down the shade.

"What's my ex-husband doing here?" Mel asked in astonishment.

"Mel, please take this case." Taylor Lawrence Archer ran his fingers through his long, black hair. Mel noted it had been professionally groomed.

"Taylor, I hate when you talk to me like that."

She had never been able to resist his charisma and witty sense of humor from the first moment they met. That sensuality filled the recycled air in the confinement of the brick-walled room.

"I can pay you," Terry interrupted.

"It isn't that," Mel said, as she backed away from the two. "I'm not the attorney here. I believe this is a significant conflict of interest for me. After all, Peter Connelly hired me first. And if the police believe you are the reason . . . that you have the missing money . . ."

"I promise you, Mel. I had nothing to do with the robbery or the problems after that. Please believe me," Terry pleaded, tears brimming her eyelids.

"Listen, you two. Peter paid me half my fee before he was murdered, and I haven't completed my assignment for him yet. I owe it to Peter to . . ."

Terry stood and laid her hand on Mel's forearm. "And I have the other half."

Mel backed away and yanked her arm away from Terry. "What?"

"Peter felt his life was in danger. So, he gave me the other piece, with instructions to give it to you if anything happened to him."

"Do you have that in writing?" Mel asked.

"No, of course not. We never thought it would come to this."

"And the police don't believe you either," Mel said.

"She really doesn't know where the bank funds are," Taylor Archer added.

"Don't fool me with those drop-dead eyes. Let her convince me." Mel gave him a look.

"Miss Walker, the police have some damning evidence against me. You must help me. I need you," Terry pleaded.

Mel faced one corner of the room, leaned against the wall, and picked at her nails. She turned to Terry and Taylor. "If the

147

one-half of the bearer bond is part of the bank loot, it's no good to anyone anyway. It'll have to be returned to the bank or their insurance company."

"That wasn't the source," Terry said.

"Where did it come from? Is it clean?" Mel asked.

Taylor smiled and slyly replied, "Why don't you and I go somewhere away from police eyes and talk about this next answer?"

❖ Chapter 28 ❖

Taylor followed Johnnie and Mel to T.J.'s. Johnnie chose a corner table facing the bay. Mel found herself looking across the small wooden table at her ex-husband's marbled black-blue eyes. He maintained the rakish smile, tight body, and winning personality that first drew them together. Even that scar above the right eyelid had sex appeal.

"Nice to see you, Taylor," Dorothea said. "What will you guys have?"

"Iced tea for me," Mel said.

"Me, too," Johnnie added.

Taylor nodded.

Dorothea set some chips and salsa in front of them and left.

"You look great, Taylor."

"Thank you, Mel. You too."

She rubbed the sleeve on his suit. "Expensive, huh?"

"Business has been very good. I hope you can drop by my new offices. Professionally decorated. The place is a knockout."

"I'll bet it is. You always did like nice things."

"New car too," Johnnie added. "I love the new Porsche. Someday I'll own one."

"You will, Johnnie," Mel replied.

"I've had a while to think about your conflict of interest

question, Mel," Taylor said.

"And . . ."

"I don't believe there is one. After all, you aren't violating anyone's interest. Peter's original assignment to you isn't clear, but it must have something to do with finding the money. Can we all agree on that point?"

Johnnie and Mel nodded their heads and munched on chips.

"Terry says she gave Peter the bond so he could hire you. So absent Peter, she becomes the fiduciary client, the extended client, so to speak."

"And, if we were to continue this investigation, what could you tell us . . . you know, respecting client privilege, that would convince us of her innocence?"

"I'll give you everything the police gave me. You'll have unlimited access to Terry and any documents she can give you. And, of course, all your written reports will be sent to me direct so they become work product."

"Taylor, I hate to bring this up, but I have a wee bit of a problem with your handling this case," Mel told him.

"Because . . .?"

"Several reasons including our history together. You're not a criminal attorney. Sometimes you're not even a good attorney and you're rarely sober."

Taylor clenched his fist and pounded the table. "Damn it, Mel. You don't know me now. I've changed."

"Forgot to mention your short, volatile fuse," Mel added.

Taylor inhaled, then leaned over and whispered to them both, "I've been in AA for six months. I'm really trying. Almost cost me my license to practice. I won't do anything to jeopardize that."

"That'd really piss me off if you did, since I put you through law school," Mel said.

"And this is the thanks I get from you? This is my chance to show you I'm clean, sober, and dependable. Together we have a good opportunity to right a wrong. Won't you help?"

Mel looked at Johnnie, then to Taylor. "One day at a time."

"Deal. Do you need an advance?" Taylor extended his right hand to Mel.

"No. We'll work time and hour, plus expenses. So give me her police file and let us get to work. I hope I don't live to regret this."

The trio walked to the trunk of Taylor's ice-blue Porsche. He pulled out a manila file-folder and handed it to Mel.

"You already had a copy of the file? You knew I'd take the case didn't you?" Mel slapped his shoulder with the folder.

"I hoped," he smiled.

"I was always a sucker for a tight ass."

"Me, too," Johnnie added.

They laughed and waved goodbye. Johnnie read the file aloud while they drove down Pacific Coast Highway.

"Okay. Her name is Terry Malone. Stands five-feet, two inches tall, one hundred two-pounds, dyed-blonde hair, brown eyes, widowed, no kids, big jugs."

"It doesn't say 'big jugs'," Mel smiled.

"Trying to get you out of the doldrums."

"Something happens when I see Taylor."

"Especially after an all-night binge."

Mel rubbed her temple. "That didn't help for sure."

"Why are you concentrating so hard?"

"I always get this way when someone is following me, and I know for sure it ain't Buddy Danko this time."

❖ Chapter 29 ❖

Mel turned off the highway and drove straight to the Harbour Pointe Police Department. Her tail followed close behind. She and Johnnie got out of the car and walked to the entrance like they were going inside. When the shadow approached the parking lot filled with black-and-white patrol cars, the driver made an abrupt U-turn and drove away. Mel and Johnnie turned around and returned to her Mercedes. She had her hand on the door handle when she heard her name.

"Mel, wait up."

"Hi, X-Ray," Johnnie said.

"What are you doing here?"

"I decided to take the Malone case and I'm thinking of talking with Terry."

"Taylor left us instructions that you could see her. That's no problem."

"Okay. We'll be back after we've had a chance to review the file and do some initial checking. Are you sure we have everything you have?"

X-Ray opened his palms facing Mel and replied, "Hey, would I hide anything from my favorite lady?"

"Yeah, you would," Mel said. She got into the car and drove to the office. This time no one followed.

❖❖❖

Mel and Johnnie knelt on dining room chairs with their elbows on the table. Several large pieces of butcher paper had been taped together making one huge continuous mural. A glass of cola and an open bag of chips lay in the middle of the picture.

"What's our first step with Terry now in the circle?" Johnnie asked.

"Why don't we run assets on her? X-Ray said he had a quote, track on the money, unquote. Let's see what he's got on her."

"On the job," Johnnie disappeared down the hall.

The phone rang.

"I'll get it," Mel said and lifted the hands-free receiver. "Walker Investigations. May I help you?"

"Hi, honey. Busy?"

"Always, Lucas. But it's so good to hear from you." Her breath quickened and her heart skipped a beat. Okay Lucas Tanner, she had to admit to herself, you must mean more to me than I've been willing to admit.

"You got back from Maui okay?"

"Good flight, as much as five hours in the air can be. How are you, honey?"

"Missing you. But working to keep me busy. You back at work?"

"Yeah. Say, I have another call coming in, can you hold just a second?"

"I can't babe. I'm on a marine line. Calling from Baku."

"What's that background noise? An oil rig?"

"No. If I didn't know better, I'd think that sounds like a

154

missile attack," he laughed.

"Rockets? Jesus, Lucas."

"Honey," he said in a serious tone, "Can I call you back in a few minutes?"

"Sure, Lucas. Shit. Hello, Walker Investigations."

"Miss Walker?"

"Yes."

"This is Dr. Reynolds' office. She asked me to call you about your recent consultation. Have you had an opportunity to think about having your work done?"

Mel shivered, remembering the body in the morgue and now concern about Lucas' safety. "Well, actually I'm working on a big case right now and haven't had much time to think about anything else. This isn't a good time right now. And I'm waiting for an important call from Europe. Why don't you give me a few more days? I'll get back to you."

"That's fine. I believe you have the rates and if money is a consideration, we'll gladly work something out for you."

"Money isn't an issue. I have a significant problem with my back," she snapped.

"Your back?"

"Yeah. I have a yellow stripe that runs the entire length."

The lady chuckled, "You are so funny."

"And so honest. Thank you for calling."

Johnnie called out from his office. "Want to see this when you're free?"

"Coming. Oh, Johnnie, you can't believe."

"What?"

"I was talking with Lucas. There were background noises that sounded like military firepower and he hung up. What do you know about Baku?"

"It's a small country. I think it was part of the original Soviet Union before the breakup. Rockets are you sure?"

"I distinctly heard sounds like in-bound missiles when we disconnected."

"Shit."

"He said he'd call me right back."

"I'm sure he's going to be all right. He'll call you back. Oh, gosh, look at this," Johnnie tried to distract Mel and pointed to the screen. "Considerable assets. We're talking high six figures here."

"I can't worry about that right now."

"It'd take your mind off something you have no control over, Mel. Besides, there's no military action in that area. It's rich in oil. I think I read where our government has sent in a group of financiers . . . working on a plan to help Baku develop their economy. Have you read anything in the papers to cause you concern?"

"No. I never heard of Baku before today, but then my focus hasn't been on a war that didn't affect me personally until now."

"I'm telling you there is no war."

"Are you sure?"

"He's gonna be okay. He'll call back. You'll see that you're worried over nothing. I think you care more about Lucas than you let on." Johnnie put his arm around Mel and kissed her cheek.

She gripped the phone receiver. "I don't know. I'm so confused right now."

"In the meantime, focus on this."

Mel looked at the monitor. "Terry does have money. When did the money first show up in her portfolio?"

"Hmm," Johnnie clicked a few keys and they waited, "Several

156

years ago."

Mel stared at the cordless phone.

"That isn't going to make it ring."

"I've got to do something to keep my mind busy. This is driving me crazy. Let's check those deposit dates against the time frame when Peter and Buddy went to prison."

"You do that and I'll get us another cold drink." Johnnie bounced up and carried his glass to the kitchen. Mel sat in his swivel chair still holding the phone.

"Look at this, will ya?" Mel said. "Terry made a big cash deposit one week after Buddy and Peter were arrested."

"Is this what X-Ray has?" Johnnie asked.

"The police department must think this deposit is the bank's money."

"Can they track the serial numbers from that date?"

"Good question, Johnnie. I don't have any idea."

"Is she sole owner of the bar?"

"Yeah."

"We need to get her tax records. Got a deep throat for that?"

"Sure."

"Inside the I.R.S.?"

"No way. But this gal's very reliable. I'll e-mail her. She has good turnaround on tax data."

"How far back can we go on Terry's taxes?"

"As far as it takes."

Mel placed the phone on the desktop, tapped the keyboard, and squinted at the monitor. The phone rang.

Johnnie answered it. "Walker Investigations, Johnnie Blake speaking. Lucas, are you okay? That noise scared the shit out of Mel. Yeah, sure. Here she is."

"Lucas?"

157

"Hi hon."

"What happened? Are you all right?"

"We're having a bit of rebel trouble here. I'm fine, but miss you."

"Thank heaven. You scared me. What rebels?"

"Honey, no matter where you go in the world, there are rebel factions."

"Was that a missile?"

"Nothing to worry about, Mel."

"Is Baku near the Gulf?"

Johnnie put one hand on his hip, cocked one shoulder forward and blew Mel an over-exaggerated kiss. Mel extended her middle finger in response.

"No. I'd feel better if it was near the Gulf."

"What are you doing there?"

"Got a contract for oil exploration from a group of Texas investors. They asked me to scope out a plan for a pipeline. Baku is a tiny country, but very rich in unexplored reserves."

"Are you alone?" Mel asked.

"I brought my Saudi crew with me."

"I miss you."

"I miss you, too. Say, I'm just finishing up with the money men and should be out of here in a few days. Wondered if you'd have time to spend if I come in say, next Saturday? I'll take the same flight I always do."

"Of course, honey."

Johnnie pointed to his arm and winced.

"Oh, yeah, and Johnnie got shot."

Johnnie sashayed out of the room. "Oh, yeah, I almost got murdered. You forgot to tell him that."

"Quit pouting," she called after Johnnie.

"What honey? I can't hear you. The phone's breaking up."

"I was just talking to Johnnie. Oh, he sends his regards."

"Send them back. You say he got shot. Is he going to be okay?"

"He'll live."

"When did it happen?"

"The evening I returned from Hawaii. We met with a new client. Someone killed the guy and Johnnie got shot."

"I don't like the sound of that. What does X-Ray say?"

"He's on the job and keeps telling me to keep my nose clean."

"For once, I agree with him. Please be careful and stay out of trouble. I'll be in Saturday. And I'll call you again if my schedule changes."

"I'll be at the airport to get you. It's wonderful to hear your voice, Lucas. *Maa alsalama.*"

"What'd you say, honey?"

"Goodbye in Farsi, maybe Arabic. I forget."

"You are amazing. Oh, my God. I . . ."

Mel heard the sounds of a massive explosion and then silence.

"Oh, shit," Mel screamed.

Johnnie rushed into the room, "What's the matter?"

"We were saying goodbye, and I heard . . . oh, my God," Mel wept and shook.

Johnnie hugged her, holding her tight. "Where, in Baku, was he calling from?"

"Someplace, I don't know where. Oh, God. What can I do?"

"Try recalling him. We've got that phone service. Dial the last-call code."

"Oh, God, I forgot." Mel dialed the numbers.

"The number you are calling is out of service. Please make sure you have the . . ."

"Shit. The number is out of order."

"Okay. Don't panic. Call X-Ray. He may have an idea."

Mel's hands shook as she called the police department. "Hello, is X-Ray in? I really need him," she pleaded. Her body quivered uncontrollably as she paced the living and dining rooms.

Johnnie took the phone from her, "Page him, please, and tell him to call Mel at the office. It's urgent." He ran to the television set and turned it on. "If this is an international incident that affects the world, *CNN* would have a news-break, don't you think?"

"Oh, that's a good idea." Mel sat cross-legged on the floor facing the set.

Neither of them spoke for several minutes as the news anchor reported continuing problems with the devaluation of the ruble in the Soviet Union.

"Come on," Mel said. "You must know something."

The phone rang.

"X-Ray?" Mel sputtered.

"Yeah. What's the problem?"

"Oh, God. Lucas called from some God forsaken place called Baku . . . twice. I heard what sounded like rockets or missiles. Something that exploded anyway. And we got disconnected after the second call. I tried to call him back and the line's dead."

"Let me call the state department. I have a friend there."

"That's a great idea. I'll be here. Please hurry."

"Mel?"

"Yeah."

"There's nothing we can do from here. Keep calm. I'll call you back."

Mel sat for a few moments watching television. "It's hard to concentrate."

"Try not to worry. I'm sure everything is okay," Johnnie said.

160

"You've got the best of two worlds right now. Your husband is sniffing around and Lucas is going to come home."

"Ex-husband . . . and he's not sniffing. We're working on a case together."

"Good. Let's stay focused. Where were we now?"

Mel turned the sound up on the television and joined Johnnie in his office.

"What else do the cops have?" Johnnie asked.

Mel read the police report. "Ug. She owns a 9mm."

"Did they find it?"

"Terry claims she had it behind the bar for protection and someone stole it."

"That's not what I asked. Is it missing?"

"More bad news. The police have it. Found it in Buddy's car."

"Shit."

"And ballistics say it's the gun used to kill Peter and shoot you."

"Double shit."

Mel flipped over another page, "And Buddy."

"Triple shit."

The phone rang.

"Mel Walker speaking."

"Is Johnnie Blake in? District Attorney's office calling."

"Let me have your number and I'll have him call you back on another line. I have an emergency and need to keep this line free."

Mel wrote the number on a telephone pad, tore the paper off, and handed it to Johnnie. She toyed with her drink and scrolled through several documents on the screen. In a few moments, Johnnie returned.

"So, can they make a connection from Terry to Buddy is the

next question?" Mel asked.

"The police took a statement from some guy who places the weapon in her rental property after she reported it stolen."

❖ Chapter 30 ❖

"Taylor, when can we talk with Terry?"

"The arraignment was this morning. She bailed and should be calling you soon to set up an appointment."

"Taylor, what's wrong with this picture? This case is simple, short, and sweet. Quarter of a million dollars stolen and that's exactly what she deposited after Peter and Buddy were arrested. The murder weapon is linked to property she owned ... after she reported the gun stolen. She lied. What else do they need?"

"They have to prove several things, Mel. That the money she deposited was from the robbery. That she knew where the gun was and used it. Her prints were not on the weapon, you know. Most importantly ... what's her motive? Why would she want Peter dead?"

"To reduce sharing it with Peter when he knew she had moved it."

"Mel, she would never do that."

"Why? What makes you so sure?"

"Because she loved Peter."

"Shit. She must be devastated. I have another question."

"Shoot."

"Where did she get that much cash to deposit if it didn't come from the robbery?"

"Mel, you'll have to ask her that yourself."

"Has X-Ray called, yet?" Johnnie asked.

"Not a word from his contact at the state department."

"Listen, sometimes no news is good news."

"I wish I could believe that. I can't seem to concentrate."

"Try. This case is getting to a critical stage. I need you to be sharp. Wow. This is amazing. Look at this."

"What did my friend get us?"

"Ten years of Terry's tax records."

"Johnnie, I've told you before, when citizens have numbers they have few secrets."

"Jesus, I believe you."

"Print it out."

"Can cops get this?"

"Not this way."

"Why didn't we just ask Terry for her tax records?"

"For one thing, I'm not sure Taylor would let me have them. Also, I don't want any surprises."

Mel and Johnnie charted Terry's income against her expenses and poured over the printouts for several hours. They compared the moving assets against the important dates in the case history. Mel had *CNN News* blaring throughout the house, but no mention was made of any activity in Baku.

Terry's phone call interrupted them.

"Taylor and I appeared in court today. He's very good, you know."

"He better be. He was a lousy husband. I'm glad to know the

law degree I funded didn't go to waste."

"I posted bail, and I'm at the Skin, if you'd like to drop by and talk."

"I would, yes. About an hour?"

"Fine. See you then."

"Johnnie, Charlotte posted Buddy's bond. See if it was our friend, Bailey who posted Terry's . . ."

He finished Mel's sentence, "Bond and how much cash she needed and what she used for collateral."

"Right. I'll be in the car. I'm going to meet her at the bar. And if X-Ray or Lucas calls . . ."

"I'll find you."

"If you leave the office forward the phone calls to me."

"Don't worry."

Mel gathered her keys, purse and cell phone. "Bye. Call me," she yelled at Johnnie.

"I'm on the job," he hollered back.

Mel drove north on Pacific Coast Highway toward Costa Mesa amid typical beach traffic. Lots of stop-and-lookers at girls in bikinis on roller blades and guys in spandex on bicycles. She stopped for a light and stared at one black-haired young woman of about twenty. The girl had visible piercings through the front of her chin below her lip, the side of one cheek, and her nose.

Her ears, in particular, fascinated Mel. The holes in the lower part of the ears had been expanded by larger and larger studs. A half-dollar could now be passed through the lobe openings. Mel shuddered as the light turned green and the phone rang.

"Speak to me oh, no pierced one," Mel said.

"What?"

"You aren't pierced anywhere, are you, Johnnie?"

"That's none of your business. Now, it appears the judge doesn't think the case is as strong as the D.A. does. Bail low, murder two, and first offense . . . a hundred thousand."

"Cash is my guess," Mel said.

"Fifty thou cash and fifty first trust deed on that home on Richelieu that we saw on her real estate records."

"And she gets that back . . .?"

"When she makes all appearances and goes to trial. The bond is exonerated, but the fifty cash . . ."

"She can kiss goodbye."

"Yeah. You know the drill."

"What are your plans this afternoon?"

"Let me finish charting and I'll bring it home tonight. Rosa called. Dinner will be waiting for us. The shoulder is bothering me. I'm going to take some pills Doc Townsend gave me, soak in the spa, and rest a bit before dinner."

"Don't overdo it. And don't mix alcohol with those drugs. No word from Lucas?"

"None. And nothing on CNN either."

"See you at home. You know where I'll be if you need me. Don't forget to refer the office calls."

"No problem. Consider it done. Bye."

Mel found a parking space behind the Skin Inn and walked through a back entrance she had not noticed before. She passed a small hallway and two men who were on the way to the bathroom. They ignored Mel, and she smiled. A Sam Cooke song played on the CD player to an empty, low-lit stage. As her eyes adjusted, she saw a new bartender. The topless woman appeared to be Middle Eastern, with silky olive skin, long black hair, large brown eyes and breasts to match. The woman looked up and spoke.

"You're Mel?" she asked with a lilting accent Mel could not place.

"Yes. Terry's expecting me."

A door opened near the end of the bar and Terry motioned for Mel to join her.

"Can I get you something to drink, Mel?" she asked.

"Anything diet."

Terry called to the bartender and walked around a large Danish-style desk to her chair. The phone rang and she answered it, giving Mel time to make mental notes of her surroundings. The brown-to-beige marble floor touched walls painted with a near-matching shade of light toast.

Despite the clutter of papers, a FAX machine ringing, and Terry talking, Mel could not keep her eyes off what appeared to be an original portrait of a stunning young woman. Long, highlighted hair cascaded in soft curls over tiny shoulders. One breast, partially exposed under a rich, royal-blue suit jacket, puffy proud lips, and . . ."

"Oh," Mel caught herself saying out loud.

A younger set of those sad cocoa-colored eyes.

"Yeah. That's me," Terry said, as she concluded her conversation.

"You are one beautiful woman."

"I was . . . once." Terry leaned back in her chair, made a tent with her fingers, and stared into the dead air somewhere beyond Mel's head.

"Tough day?"

"Tough life. But," Terry leaned forward and balanced her elbows on the desktop, "I brought a lot of this on myself."

"We all make choices, Terry. Some of them are better than others. The important thing is to learn from our mistakes and not repeat the past."

The bartender knocked on the door, entered, and laid Mel's drink on a white plastic coaster. She left the room and closed the door behind her.

"The only gentle man I ever knew and loved is gone. And I'm accused of murdering him and indirectly causing death and injury to others. I have nothing to gain and nothing to live for now." Terry dropped her head into a cradle of her arms and sobbed, "Nothing."

Mel stood, walked around the desk and gently rubbed Terry's arms. "I know what you must be feeling . . ."

Terry looked at Mel through tear-stained eyes. "What could you possibly know about losing someone?"

"Girl friend," Mel said, with both hands on her hips. "Do we have a lot to talk about!"

❖ Chapter 31 ❖

Mel wiped the edges of her mouth with a paper napkin and leaned back in her dining room chair. Johnnie nibbled on the last kernels of corn-on-the-cob and sighed.

"That Rosa," she said, after a few seconds of silence. "She is one fabulous cook."

"Lucas missed a fine southern meal."

"I pray he ate dinner somewhere safe tonight."

"Me too."

"You think he's looking at the same moon we are?"

"I sure do." He reached over and squeezed her hand.

"Maybe I'll cook for him when he comes in."

Johnnie stacked the dishes and silverware and took them to the kitchen. "How much is that gonna cost me?"

"What?"

"I'd pay good money to see you cook. Good money."

Mel wiped the tabletop and joined him in the kitchen. "Smart-ass. I can cook."

"When?"

"When I'm inspired." Mel swatted his butt with the end of a cheesecloth towel.

"Well, I'm ready to hear all about your meeting with Terry today. How about some coffee?"

Mel poured two cups and stepped onto the patio. "Ah, just in time for a glorious sunset."

"I'll drink to that," Johnnie said, reaching for his cup.

"Terry has a very interesting story. I'm not sure I believe all of it, but let's try it on for size."

"Shoot."

"Terry Malone has the kind of story that only a poet could write. Poor at birth. Poor in love. She is the youngest of eight girls, born to a sharecropper in Mississippi. Wore hand-me-down clothes, picked peas for two cents a pound 'til her fingers bled, and attended a one-room school. Father spared no rod on any female in the house. He worked hard and expected no less from his kids. Government subsidized the farm and Mom socked away some money. When the old man's liver gave out, she sold the farm, moved to the city, bought a bar, and put the girls to work."

"Vertically and horizontally?"

"You got it."

"I have the picture. Terry lost her virginity early and married the first man who said, 'I love you. Let me take you away from all this'."

"Only . . ."

"He was the new town drunk."

"Won the title hands-down, after her dad died."

Johnnie sang, "I want a man, just like the man who battered dear old Mom."

"Who also inherited the proud titles . . ."

"Town bully and wife beater."

"Interesting though, Mom had a life insurance policy. She drove off a lonely graveled road after a three-day binge and left an imprint of her head on a tree, and . . ."

"Set the girls free."

170

"Armed with her share of insurance proceeds and money from the sale of the bar, Terry drops the sisters, one-by-one, as they marry other losers, drunks, and abusers. She catches the first bus west and opens a club called Dizzie's Dolls. It's a cash cow. Exotic dancers pay her to work there. Terry's bringing in large sums of cash and socking it back. She decides to remodel and an electrician starts a fire and . . ."

"Insurance proceeds move her up to door number three."

"Yeah. Now here's the good part."

"There's good news? Wait, I need more coffee." Johnnie dashed inside and returned with the coffee pot. "Okay. Continue."

"She builds the Skin Inn, joins the Chamber of Commerce, and makes large contributions to MADD."

"Ms. Community Leader."

"Looking for Mr. Right, when . . ."

"Buddy brings Peter into the bar."

"Tries like hell to talk them out of robbing the bank. She loves Peter madly. Offers him title to the bar."

"Shit."

"He was determined to rob the bank."

"And he gets caught."

"She's been stashing cash all over town for years. After he's arrested, she deposits two hundred fifty thousand cash for his bail without thinking through all the consequences."

"And he cops a plea and goes to prison?"

"She took a great risk exposing this cash because . . .?"

"Because?"

"The I.R.S. She never disclosed all this cash income."

"So, how do we prove it?"

"We might try adding her overhead and expenses, vendors,

supplies, et cetera, plus the values of her known and unrecorded assets to show she had cash she didn't declare."

"In other words, demonstrate reasonable doubt for the source of the funds."

"Exactly. It'll give her a huge tax liability."

"Well, that's better than a murder conviction."

"I think I can save us a lot of legwork. Got an idea."

"How? What?" Johnnie asked.

"Now that we know she hid money, how about if I simply ask her for her second set of books?"

❖ Chapter 32 ❖

The distant grinding of a lawnmower engine hammered Mel's head when she rolled over the next morning. The grating noise caused her to yawn and stretch into consciousness.

She showered, dressed in jeans and a freshly ironed T-shirt, and joined Rosa and Johnnie in the kitchen where they chattered away.

"You know, I don't do mornings. Where's my caffeine?"

Rosa handed Mel a cup of coffee. "Johnnie told me about Lucas. Any word?"

"Not yet. X-Ray's still working on it."

"Did you try that phone number again?" Johnnie asked.

"Yeah. It's still out of order."

"Did you forget?" Rosa whispered. "You forgot. I knew you would."

"What?" Mel asked. "Forget what?"

"Today is *Casa Angeles'* annual garage sale. You said you'd help."

"I'm really busy what with Lucas and this case, Rosa. How much money do you need?"

"Anybody can write a check. Don't get me wrong, contributions are important. But today you said you'd come with me, meet the other volunteers, and help out with the sale. Besides

173

you need a break." Rosa stood feet apart with hands on her hips, the picture of authority.

"It's time you got involved in something besides work," Johnnie said.

"Don't you have any friends who could join us?" Rosa asked.

"Women don't like to be reminded that battery and abuse exist. It's not a pleasant subject."

"One of America's great secrets we stuff under the beds, huh?"

"Right." Mel sipped coffee and ate dry toast. "Also, we're working a big case that's going to require a lot of fast turnaround. And I want to be near a telephone."

"I've got the perfect volunteer," Johnnie said, excitedly. "She could use a friend and it might help us get what we want."

Mel looked up from toying with the breadcrumbs. Her eyes sparkled as the idea developed. "Perfect. I'll call her." She left the breakfast room and picked up the kitchen phone.

"Who's that she gonna call?" Rosa asked.

"We have a client fresh out of jail on a murder charge."

"Johnnie, we don't need more criminals in our program. A battered women and children's shelter is not the place for a murderer."

He stood and waved his hands. "No, no. She's a very nice lady. Mel and I like her and she could be innocent. The woman's been beaten her entire life. You'll love her. I promise." He crossed his heart.

"Anonymity is the keyword in protecting the victims at *Casa Angeles.*" A woman spoke from the porch of a small, white-frame home on a residential street in downtown Long Beach. She continued, "So that today's sale will be an unqualified success, all our friends, including the volunteers, will alternate personnel in the sales booths. God has granted us fabulous weather. Good luck, ladies and gentlemen."

Polite but enthusiastic applause filled a front yard cluttered with chairs, sofas, clothes, and toys.

Johnnie patted a calico stray that wandered in and around human legs. "I miss Scat."

"I miss Lucas," Mel added.

"Me too. But they'll both come home safe and sound. You'll see," Rosa said.

Terry drove up in a red Mercedes. Mel greeted her. Johnnie hugged her and introduced Terry to Rosa. Terry wore blue-jean shorts and a laundered denim shirt tied at the waist. Her long hair flowed from under a blue silk scarf. A light touch of makeup and toast-colored lipstick completed the picture. Today she looked like an ordinary person in regular clothes.

"Mel, I don't mind telling you I was surprised to hear from you. But I'm very excited at the prospect of sharing a day away from the bar, with new friends . . . helping others."

"We're glad you could come," Johnnie smiled.

Rosa, Johnnie, Mel, and Terry stood side-by-side facing a volunteer who gave them instructions. "Negotiate is the key to selling," the gray-haired woman said. "But we're here to move the items, not to store them." She clapped her hands and dismissed the troops.

The sun warmed the energy around them, and Mel caught Rosa and Terry more than once, giggling in conspiracy over a sale. Terry would take pieces of old silk flowers and a cheap pottery vase that hadn't sold and make a centerpiece

175

arrangement that sold immediately. Terry made up stories of pure fiction on the item's chain of ownership, often creating a bidding war among prospective buyers.

At midday, Rosa pulled a large wicker basket from the Pumpkin's trunk and the four ate and laughed under a large olive tree in the backyard. By early afternoon the yard sale had been deemed a success and the organizers thanked everyone for their unselfish efforts.

Terry walked over to the organizer and pressed an envelope into her hands as they talked. Mel watched from a safe distance, not wanting to encroach on Terry's privacy. Instead, Mel joined Rosa and Johnnie loading a chair and some pillows that Johnnie bought for his apartment.

"This has been the most wonderful day of my life. Thank you, Mel," Terry said. "Johnnie, Rosa, you don't know what today has meant to me."

Mel joined the group hug that included Rosa, Johnnie, and Terry. "We need to talk about your case when you have a minute," she said, withdrawing from the circle.

"Anything. Anytime."

"I hope you mean it," Johnnie said.

Mel turned to see if they had forgotten anything. The *Casa Angeles* organizer opened the envelope, read a note inside, unfolded what appeared to be a check, looked at Terry, and began to cry. Mel smiled.

"I hope this will be the start of good things for all of us." Terry waved goodbye, got in her car, and drove off.

"Mel," Rosa said, "that was no murderess. I watch TV. I know killers. Anyway, I've invited her to dinner tomorrow."

❖ Chapter 33 ❖

"What do you think you're doing, Mel?" Taylor asked.

"Conducting the investigation you hired me to do. What's your problem?"

"Bringing her second set of books into evidence opens Terry to tremendous tax liabilities, costly financial penalties, and possible imprisonment."

"Do you have any other ideas how we might prove the source of her funds?"

"Not right now."

"Neither do I. But taxes, as much as I hate them, are a hell of a lot better punishment than being someone's girl friend in Tehachapi."

"What's that?"

"The woman's prison north of Los Angeles."

"Let me think on it."

"You do that. Remember, we're only reporting to you for now. What you decide to do with the information is your business, counselor. In the meantime, I'll get the review done, the books indexed and tabbed, and get you a captioned report."

"Ever efficient. I miss you, honey."

"By the way, how are you and Natalie doing?"

"As the trial drew to a close, we drifted further apart. I had to leave the law firm. I guess my attraction wasn't as great as it might have appeared. I hear she's dating a new guy in the firm. He's the nephew of another partner."

"Bummer."

"I really miss you."

"Any port in the storm, as they say."

"No. It's nothing like that. I've dated, now and then, but nothing serious. Baby, I've changed. Really turned my life around. I hope you'll give me a chance to come back into your life again."

"One day at a time, Taylor. Dating an ex-husband is not a priority for me. I have other personal issues bothering me right now. Let me finish this assignment. Strictly business, okay?"

"For now, I'll agree to that."

"Taylor, you don't have a choice. That was not an option. So get back to me, if you think of another way to prove the source of her funds. Johnnie and I have run through every other possible scenario we can think of."

"Fine. I understand Terry's coming to your home for dinner tonight. I'll tell her to bring the books."

"And any other secrets she may wish to share with us."

Mel and Johnnie busied themselves with other cases at the office throughout the day. At five o'clock Mel locked the office and Johnnie followed her home. Before they neared her gated entrance, Mel's cell phone rang.

"Speak," she said.

"This is interesting," Johnnie said.

"I'll bite."

"I'm following you. So, who's following me?"

Mel moved the steering wheel slightly over the center line. Johnnie steered the Pumpkin to the shoulder.

"I see it. Looks like the same dark sedan that followed us to the police department the other day. Can you see if it's a man or woman driving?"

"Nope. Tinted windows."

"Any passengers?"

"Ditto."

"So, slow down, pretend to park or turn off. I'll speed up. Let it pass you. Then move into position, and let's cap 'em and get the license plate number."

"What's a 'cap'?"

"What insurance scam artists do when they set up phony car accidents. One car gets ahead and the other drops back. They put the pigeon between them."

"Got it, *Kemo Sabe.*"

Johnnie clicked the turn signal on and slowed as they passed a small shopping strip. Mel hit the accelerator and glanced in the rear view mirror. The mysterious car jumped ahead of Johnnie. Mel hit the brakes and the sedan was now wedged tightly between them. Mel copied the number from the Arizona license plate, slowed, and turned into her private gate.

Once inside the house Johnnie and Mel hi-fived each other on getting the license number.

Johnnie said, "Who do we know in Colorado who'd follow us?"

"Colorado? The front plate was Arizona."

"Shit. The plates were probably stolen. But just in case, I'll run 'em both on DMV."

"Rosa, we're home," Mel called out.

179

The pungency of saffron filled her nostrils as she dropped her purse at the bottom of the stairway and joined Rosa in the kitchen. She hugged Rosa, "Oh, my favorite. *Paella.* You've been cooking all day."

"Not cooking, just preparing," Rosa corrected her. "It's the damn cleaning, slicing, dicing, and precooking everything to get it ready for that last twenty minutes . . . that's a bitch."

"Can I set the table?"

"No thanks. That's been done. I'm saving you for the dishes."

"Hmm, *paella*," Johnnie said, entering the room. He raised the skillet lid and picked at chunks of fish with his fingers.

Rosa swatted him with a wooden spoon. "Stay out of that. It's not ready yet."

"Can I set the table?" Johnnie asked.

Mel rushed her answer, "Maybe you can do the dishes for us."

She and Rosa laughed. As Mel proceeded to the bar and poured a drink, the phone rang.

"Hi. Yes, we're expecting her. Thank you." Mel turned to Johnnie. "Terry's at the gate."

Johnnie opened the front door and greeted Terry, who carried a bottle of white wine. Mel joined them and hugged Terry. Rosa wiped her hands on a white tea-towel she had wrapped around her waist, pushed a curl off her forehead, and waited her turn.

"Would you like a drink before dinner?" Johnnie asked.

"I'm fine for now. Just wine with dinner."

Terry wore a bright print sun dress. A hot-pink silk bow set off her long curls. Pewter-gray sandals accented her pink, painted toenails.

"You look beautiful," Mel said.

"Thank you. I needed that." Terry smiled at her.

"We all do. Come join us. Rosa's been preparing dinner all day for us."

They ate, talked, laughed, and told stories like old friends until Johnnie began scraping dried yellow rice from the bottom of the pan.

"I know this isn't good manners, Rosa, but that was delicious and I wouldn't hurt your feelings."

"You'll please the chef even more when you do the dishes," Rosa said. "I hate to eat and run, but I've got a family waiting for me. And you must have business to conduct."

They said goodbyes while Johnnie stacked the dishes and carried them to the kitchen. Terry called out to him, "I'll do the dishes if you'll unload my car."

Johnnie dropped the towel on the counter, took her keys, and whispered to Mel on his way out the front door, "Nana, Na, Na, Na, Na."

"Don't you need some help lifting heavy things?" Mel asked.

"I'm fine." Johnnie flexed his muscles at her.

Mel poured a glass of sherry for each of them and carried them out to the patio. Johnnie and Terry joined her moments later.

"You won't believe what I just unloaded from her car."

"What?"

"Boxes. Lots of boxes. You're going to find out what great record-keepers crooks are," Terry answered for him.

Two drinks later, Mel found the courage. "Terry, can we talk about Peter?"

"Sure."

"Did you know Peter Connelly had an alias, Paul Cooper?"

"Yes, I did."

"We also found papers in his home on another potential alias, a David Erickson."

"Right. We looked at both of those names, Paul Cooper and David Erickson, and decided on Cooper. I guess Peter forgot to throw away the other birth certificate and driver's license."

"Why did he go to all the trouble of taking a dead man's name, if he was still going to live in the area where he was arrested? He'd be around his mother and still see his old friends."

"He had a very bad experience in prison. He wouldn't talk with me about it. But he got involved in something. Maybe a fight . . . I don't know. He received a serious burn on his face."

"Is that why he had plastic surgery? To remove it?" Mel asked.

"The scar had thickened. Keloid, I think they call it. Peter felt he was marked for life. He wanted to have some work done to make him more attractive and reduce the scar at the same time. Maybe he felt a new name and face would give him a new lease on life."

"Put all the sadness behind him," Johnnie said.

"Right. We wanted a fresh start together. He was so gentle. I wish you two had the opportunity to know him. What a wonderful man." Terry turned her head toward the ocean, sighed, and cleared her throat.

"Can I ask you a personal question?" Mel asked.

"At this time tomorrow Mel, you and Johnnie will know more about me than my OB-GYN does. Shoot."

"In your business you see a lot of plastic surgery, don't you?"

Terry cupped her fine-pointed breasts, "Best boobs money can buy."

Johnnie put his hands over his eyes.

"What do you want to ask?"

"I'm thinking of having a little work done."

"It all started when she found a gray hair," Johnnie said.

Terry laughed. "Oh, Mel. I've got a great hairdresser who has a simple, less painful fix for that."

Mel put her index fingers next to her eyes and pulled the skin back. "What about that?"

"What she's trying to tell you," Johnnie said, "is that she got an estimate for the work last week."

Terry waved one hand at Mel. "Forget surgery. You've got a very pretty face and a nice body. These minor changes in your facial lines are normal. Don't worry too early."

"I want to do something before it gets too late."

"I'm hoping that you and I will be friends for a long time. I'll be around to tell you when you need it. And then I'll introduce you to the perfect doctor. The one all my girls use."

"Who's that?"

"Dr. Sarah Reynolds."

❖ Chapter 34 ❖

"Taylor, Johnnie and I have spent two exhaustive days on Terry's records. Everything's ready for her defense," Mel said.

"So, I guess you've answered the burning question. Did she kill anyone?"

"If she did, and I don't believe she did, it wasn't over money. She's extremely wealthy."

"How wealthy?"

"Taylor, let's just say it's almost vulgar."

"Wow."

"Where does this leave us though?"

"What do you mean?"

"Who killed Peter and Buddy? And where is the bank's money?"

"Oh."

"Do you have a trial date yet?"

"Yes, but if we can go over the work you've done, maybe I can short-circuit this by talking to the D.A. and getting the charges against Terry dismissed."

"That'd be wonderful and certainly worth a try."

"Are you available to go over the report with me?"

"Me? No. Let me get Johnnie on the phone. I'll send him with the material. I need to focus on the next piece in this puzzle."

"Which is what?"

"I have absolutely no idea."

In preparation for his trip to Taylor's downtown Los Angeles office, Johnnie filled the Pumpkin with Terry's documents, the charts, and tabbed notebooks. When Johnnie returned to the house, Mel and Rosa were drinking coffee.

"So, I'm locked, loaded, and ready to go. Where should I catch up with you?"

"I've got a few errands to run after breakfast. Then I'll be at the office. If I'm not there. I'll leave you a message."

"Do you have any new ideas?"

"Johnnie, I don't have any old ones."

The car phone rang, as Mel pulled into the office driveway.

"Mel Walker."

"Hi, it's Terry. I hope you don't mind. Rosa gave me your number."

"Not at all. How are you this morning?"

"Well-rested, thank you. Rosa is a wonderful cook and a great lady. You're lucky to have so many friends."

"You will be too, if you stick with us."

"What's that mean?"

"You didn't kill anyone." Mel shut the engine off and took the phone with her into the office. Sobs could be heard through the receiver. "Terry, don't cry. Everything's going to be fine."

185

"No one ever believed or trusted in me before."

"Well, you've got an entire flock of folks who do now."

"Where do we go from here?"

"Johnnie is on his way to see your attorney. Call Taylor later today, after he and Johnnie have had an opportunity to go over our presentation. Taylor will tell you his plan of attack."

"Can't you tell me now?"

"Terry, I'm not an attorney. My job is to gather facts, analyze them, and report to your counsel."

"I'm trying to be patient. This is so hard. I miss Peter so much."

"Believe me, I understand what you're going through."

"Anything you want to share with me?"

"Thank you, no. Just personal issues of my own. You shouldn't have to wait much longer."

"Taylor is an aggressive attorney?"

"Very."

"I'm so lucky to have found you both."

Mel removed a cold drink from the refrigerator, checked for phone messages, and flipped on her computer.

So where do I go from here? I have overlooked something crucial. I miss you Lucas. Where are you and what is the key to this riddle?

She pulled butcher paper, tacks, and two marker pens from a closet and spread a huge piece of the roll on the floor. Mel bit on one of the markers and stared at the older pieces taped together and tacked on the wall above her. Methodically, she began to transpose those circles onto the new paper.

Inside the circles she printed the names of Peter, Buddy, Terry, and the Skin Inn. She stood and tore the sheets from the wall, crumpled them up, and tossed them in the trash. The phone rang.

"Walker Investigations, Mel Walker speaking."

"X-Ray Ramirez with the Harbour Pointe Police Department. Remember me? Where have you been hiding?"

"Not hiding. Working. Any news for me on Lucas, yet?"

"None, hon. My state department contact tells me everything in that country is fine, as far as he can learn from his sources."

"You'll call, won't you?"

"You know it. Working on a new case?"

"Nope, an old one. Peter Connelly's murder."

"Working any specific issues?"

"Yeah, the 'Terry Malone is innocent' issue."

"Come on Mel. That was a slam-dunk closure. We have the money, a motive, and the weapon."

"You have some hard-earned money, an ordinary gun whose mere ownership is not proof, and no motive. You can pull that case out of 'closed' and keep looking, X. You got nothing."

"What did you find?"

"I'll leave the 'dog and pony show' to Taylor. He'll take it to the D.A.'s office."

"When will he present it?"

"You'll have to ask him. Give him a while though. Johnnie's on his way right now to Taylor's office with our report."

"Assuming for a moment that you're right, do you have any new theories for me?"

"And try to tell you how to do your job? You know me better than that, little brother."

Mel reviewed every folder she had on everyone who knew someone in the case. At one point, when analyzing street addresses, two addresses appeared in the same zip code. Mel checked her *Thomas Guide*, a book of street maps every good investigator carried to get around an ever changing Greater Southern California. The properties appeared to be several blocks apart in the Tustin Hills. She scribbled a note with the page numbers from the guide, and a second note to Johnnie:

Gone to the Orange County Building Department to check permits. No word on Lucas yet.

She sped through traffic toward the Orange County government building center.

Inside, Mel asked for the history of the building permits on several addresses, reviewing Terry's first. A curious cross-reference note with a code stamped on one corner caused Mel to raise an eyebrow. She tapped the counter top with her fingers until she got a clerk's attention.

"Excuse me," Mel said. "Can you tell me what this coding means?"

The man took off his glasses and squinted at the paper. "It means work was done on joint properties. And this number is the lot, section, and page number for the other property."

"If I gave you another address can you check to see if it's the one that corresponds to the cross-referenced number?"

"Sure. It'll take a minute. Someone's using our only microfilm."

"This isn't on computer?"

"This is Orange County. Don't you remember, because of some screwy investments, we're bankrupt. We're lucky to make payroll." The clerk laughed and walked away, taking the document with him.

People conducted business and left. Ten minutes passed.

"Got it," the man appeared, waving a paper. "You're right about one thing."

"Which is?" Mel asked.

"I've ordered the plans for one home so you can see for yourself. I didn't know they did this in California."

"Do what?"

A young man walked up to the counter and unrolled the two plans.

"Thank you," the older man said, as he balanced weights on each corner and motioned to Mel. "Come here and let's take a look."

"My God. There's a tunnel connecting Terry's home to the home on the next street. Who owns that house?" Mel scanned the addresses she had with her, but none matched the house number. "Can you tell when this tunnel was built?"

"Looks like 1981."

"Can I have a copy of these records?"

"For a few bucks and a lot of time, you can have anything copied. It'll take a while, because the big photocopier is down and we're waiting for the repairman."

"I'll be back. I need to go to the real estate records department. Copy all these." Mel waved at both sets of plans, ran down the stairs, and across the campus's green lawn to the Real Estate Division.

"Hi, Jerry. Long time, huh?" she said, breathing hard.

"Not since you got your fancy computer. Did you break it? What brings you here?"

"Building department's making some copies for me. I need to look at an address. Can you do it for me?"

"For you, Mel, anything."

Mel knew from the computer real estate data and the income tax records that Terry lived on Richelieu Street in Tustin Hills. Contractors with visions of individualism had designed this upscale Orange County community with oversized lots, dirt-filled horse trails, and massive eucalyptus trees. No two houses were alike in color, style, or size, unlike those in the adjacent cities.

The house with the tunnel to Terry's home had been built by one such contractor and was currently owned by an accounting firm.

She thanked Jerry, jumped into her car, and drove to the street behind Richelieu. Mel pulled up to the curb several houses away from the tunnel-house and parked. Time for a little witness canvas, Mel thought, as she walked up to the front door of the corner house and knocked.

Sue was the only name that came to Mel's mind when a woman opened the front door. "Hello, my name is Sue."

Mel had only a moment to size her up. Middle of the day, home in a tattered robe, mousey brown hair, not combed, no makeup, noise from a soap opera blasting through the house, and a cigarette dangling from the side of her lips. A bored housewife.

"Your neighbor at," Mel fumbled through some blank pages, "16255 Thompson has applied for an insurance policy, and it's our job to canvass the area to make sure the applicant isn't doing anything hazardous that would increase their chances of mortality."

"I hate insurance companies." The woman took a drag on the cigarette, inhaled long and deep. "They never pay any of their claims."

"Some do have terrible payment records. But not our company." Mel smiled and shifted from one foot to another.

"What do you want to know about 'em?" the woman asked.

"Do you know how many people, adult and children, live in the house?"

"Yeah, a couple of adults."

"Do they race cars, jump from planes, or do any unusual activities when they're not working?"

"Not to my knowledge. Nice quiet folks. Keep to themselves a lot."

"Do you know what the people do for a living?"

"Yeah." She scratched her head for information. "Maybe one's a doctor of some kind. The other wears a suit during the week and drives a new sports car."

"Both of them are professional types?" Mel asked.

"Yeah. As I recall, one of them is maybe a dentist, or at least works in a doctor's office."

"And the other?"

"I don't remember what that one does. They're gone an awful lot for professional folks, you know."

"Is the dentist a male or female?"

"Male. They're both quite handsome men."

At the next house no one responded to her knock. As she walked down the sidewalk to the next house a white BMW convertible with the top down swerved into the driveway and came to an abrupt stop.

"Can I help you?" A blonde woman in a tennis dress lifted her racket and purse from behind the front seat and approached Mel.

"Hi, my name is Sue. I work for an insurance company, and it's my job to verify that one of your neighbors isn't doing any hazardous work."

"You want to know this because . . .?" the lady asked, as she lifted her sunglasses.

"Oh, sorry. I'm a trainee, and I forget I'm supposed to tell you." Mel chuckled, "Your neighbor at 16255 Thompson has applied for a rather large life insurance policy. This is a very routine thing we do . . . you know, checking it out."

"Well, the one guy is a doctor, but I don't know his name. He plays tennis at our club sometimes. But, he's not on the circuit."

"Just plays for fun, huh?"

"He's not very good at it," she confided.

"Do either of the men do any hazardous things?"

"Like movie stunt work, that kind of thing?" the blond asked.

"Yeah, race cars or yachts, have a pilot's license, bungee jump?"

"Not those queens."

Mel approached the infamous tunnel-house at 16255 Thompson and knocked, not because she hoped someone would answer, but because the tennis lady was watching from across the street where she retrieved her mail.

Be cool. Please don't anyone answer this door.

When Mel arrived home, she found several messages from Rosa:

Dinner ready. Cold turkey.

No word from Lucas. I'm sure he's okay.

Johnnie called. He has a date. Catch you later.

Call X-Ray.

No Scat yet.

Terry invited us to a party at her business.

Mel wondered if Rosa or Johnnie had ever been to a topless bar.

Well, they're going now, she chuckled.

She pulled a plate covered with foil from the refrigerator, poured herself a glass of milk, and carried them to her study. She clicked on both computer and monitor, entered her password, and munched on dinner while the machine warmed up. Mel tapped the keyboard one-handed until she finished her last bite and wiped her hands on a piece of scrap paper.

Well past midnight and several search engines later, Mel thought, the puzzle will not be answered tonight.

She set the alarm and went to bed. Getting to sleep became another project. She tossed and turned, wondering who was following her and why. Where is Lucas? Why doesn't he call?

The phone rang just after she dozed off. Mel answered and the line clicked off. She got out of bed, pulled her Beretta out of the handbag, laid it under her pillow, and promptly fell asleep.

Changes in the atmosphere and temperature caused the house to creak and moan throughout Mel's restless night. By morning her less than happy enthusiasm for mornings worsened at first light, when the phone startled her into consciousness.

"This better be important," she said, after grappling to find the receiver.

"Oh honey, did I wake you? I never get these time changes right."

She scratched her head vigorously behind one ear and screamed, "Oh Lucas, where've you been? I've been worried sick.

Are you okay?"

"I'm fine. The U.N. forces evacuated all the non-natives. I'm calling from London."

"I don't care where you're calling from, so long as you're not hurt."

"I wasn't injured. Boy, do I have a story to tell you when I get home."

Mel began to cry.

"How 'bout you? Why are you crying?"

"Don't mind me. I cry when I'm grouchy and don't get enough sleep."

"A case got you down?"

"Yeah. One's a murder. The other is a case of being scared out of my mind worrying where you were, and if you were alive or not."

"Well, now you know. Everything's fine. Say, you do care about me, huh?"

"You may not know me well, but you understand me better than my ex-husband ever did. Wait a minute. Was that a guess?"

"Yeah. Just lucky, I guess."

"You devil. So you're in London?"

"Yep. Should be back in the States by the weekend. Any chance I could drop by California on my way to Texas? I'd love to see you."

"I need to hold you."

"Me too."

"I've been invited to a party. But, I'm sure Terry wouldn't mind my bringing a date. On second thought, maybe I don't want you to go."

"Why is that?"

"The party's to be held in a topless bar."

194

"Honey, when you've seen one, you've seen them both."

"Bars?"

Lucas laughed, "No silly, boobs. Party sounds like fun. Get back to sleep and I'll call you Friday if my arrival time changes."

"I'm awake, and anyway it's time to get up. There's a lot of work to do. I've got to find some money, somewhere."

"Honey, I'll loan you some money."

"Lucas, it ain't that kind of money."

❖ Chapter 35 ❖

Mel dragged herself into the shower and let the hot water beat the back of her head. She swallowed two aspirins, filled a plastic mug with coffee, and drove to the office.

Johnnie danced his Fred Astaire imitation with a broom while humming something Gershwin, off-key.

"Oh, good. You got laid," Mel said, as she opened the door, balancing the mug and her briefcase.

"Oh, he is so cute. I'm dying to tell you."

"Can you die later and quieter? I got a couple of hang-ups during the night. Lucas woke me at dawn and I've got a screaming headache to boot."

Johnnie propped the broom against one wall and walked behind her and massaged her head and neck. "Poor Mel, doesn't do dawns, does she?" he whispered.

"No."

Suddenly realizing what Mel said, Johnnie screamed, "Lucas called? What'd he say?"

"He's fine. He called from London. The United Nations got all the foreigners safely out of Baku. Isn't that wonderful?"

"Fabulous." Johnnie clapped his hands together.

"And he'll be home this weekend."

"Wonderful. Even better. You can get laid too."

❖❖❖

Johnnie gave Mel his report. "Taylor told me he'd meet with the district attorney's office today and, if all goes well, Terry's case may be dismissed."

"So you don't think the party is a bit premature?"

"A party is a party. Do you think she'll mind if I bring my new friend?" Johnnie asked.

"Probably won't hurt to call her. I'd like to take Lucas."

"Are we going to wrap up this case over the weekend? I've been invited to Big Bear."

"We're never going to solve it until I make the first domino fall."

"I don't ever recall having such a weird case. But when we get this all unraveled, the clues will make perfect sense, won't they?"

"I hope so."

Mel circled the LAX arrival lanes twice until she spotted Lucas standing at the curb. He wore black jeans, boots, and a white cotton shirt with the sleeves rolled up. He stood with his broad shoulders back, feet apart, as his fingers brushed a curl from his forehead. His hair was longer than she remembered. He was the kind of man men turned to stare at.

She pulled the car to the curb and called out, "Hi, handsome. Looking for a good time?"

A large group of people stopped on cue awaiting his response.

"How much?" Lucas replied without hesitation.

The crowd looked at Mel.

"Whatever you got cowboy and from the stretch of your jeans, it looks like plenty."

Lucas blushed as his long lanky legs brought him to the passenger door. He dropped his soft-sided carryall in the space behind the front seats, opened the door with the other hand, slid in beside Mel, and kissed her.

The airport crowd stared in amazement as Mel and Lucas drove off laughing all the way to his Orange County condo.

Her doorbell rang promptly at seven. Mel sprinted in response. Lucas wore black slacks, a black silk shirt with a Newman collar and full sleeves.

"Zorro without the cape," was Mel's first impression.

"And you," Lucas held his arms out, palms up. "Wow!"

Mel wore a red silk blouse with matching palazzo pants and low-heel, red-silk pumps. Her natural curly hair lay in soft ringlets around her face.

Mel and Lucas kissed and held each other, swaying slightly back and forth without talking.

"You ain't seen nothing yet, Texas."

"Do we have to go to this party?"

"You're turning down a chance to see topless dancers?"

He held her close and whispered, "I have my own table dancer right here." Lucas kissed the top of her ear, which sent goose-bumps down her body.

"You have this thing about you . . . that drives women wild," Mel whispered.

"Yeah. I know. But I only bring it out for special people."

"And I'm one of them?"

"You're all of them, darling."

"Johnnie, don't forget the alarm when you leave," she called out. "I've got to stop by the office."

"No problem. I'll be right behind you. I need to drive to Long Beach for my date. See you there," Johnnie replied.

Mel clutched her handbag and shoved Lucas out the front door. "If we don't go now, we'll never get there."

❖ Chapter 36 ❖

A massive wooden sign, mounted on a footed base, stood at the end of the parking-lot entrance announcing, "Private Celebration." Female valets wearing black shorts that didn't cover their rear-ends and short-sleeved white blouses exposing their ample bosoms dashed back and forth across the parking area.

Two approached Lucas' car, one on each side, as they opened the front doors.

"Welcome to the Skin Inn. May we have your names?"

"Mel Walker and guest," Lucas replied.

One woman repeated it into a walkie-talkie she carried, waited for a reply, broke into a broad grin, and said, "You're the reason we're here, Miss Walker. Go right in." She made a bold sweeping gesture toward the door, jumped into the driver's seat and drove off.

Strains from the "Barbra Streisand Broadway Album" filled the room, as Mel and Lucas moved past the silver lamé curtain into the bar. Fifty or so guests huddled in small groups and talked. Several dancers were on the stage teaching undulating stomach exercises. Mel laughed and called out through the noise, "Auditioning for a new job, Johnnie?"

"Hi, Mel," he waved, and screeched, "Hi, Lucas. It's good to see you."

Lucas gave Mel an "is Johnnie for real" look and waved back. "Hi, Johnnie. Nice to see you, too."

Mel spotted Terry near the bar, started toward her, then turned, and clenched Lucas' hand. They maneuvered their way across the floor. Terry saw them. She raised an eyebrow and held her shoulders squarely back. Her breasts pointed straight ahead. She wore a flimsy see-through skin-toned blouse. This motion did not escape Mel.

She turned and hollered into Lucas' ears, "I not only have to compete with gay men here tonight; I have to compete with exotics."

"No, you don't," he said, as he drew her near his side with a tight finger-squeeze. "I'm still here."

Terry hugged Mel, then released her and extended her right hand to Lucas. "Do you both know how lucky you are to have found each other in this crazy world? I'm Terry Malone."

"Lucas Tanner."

"Oh God, that drawl. Could you die?" Terry smiled.

"Not yet," Mel replied.

"Well, the really great news is . . ."

"Hi, Mel. Everyone." Taylor entered the circle. He shook hands with Lucas and said, "I'm sure we met somewhere before. At the American Trial Lawyers Association luncheon perhaps?"

"Taylor, this is Lucas, my date, and definitely not an attorney."

"When did we meet?" Taylor shook his head.

"I'm Patty Dotson's cousin. I was Mel's escort at Patty's Christmas boat-parade party. I vividly remember meeting you. We spilled a drink down the front of your date's cleavage."

Terry joined in the laughter that followed.

202

"Right. Right," Taylor said. "Say, Mel doesn't normally have repeat dates. That's some kind of record."

"I take that as a compliment."

"You should."

As more bodies pressed into the ever widening circle, Johnnie cried out, "Oh, is this wonderful? All my friends are here." He hugged Taylor, Mel, then Terry. He held Lucas at arm's length a second and said, "What the hell? Hug me, you hunk," and embraced him.

A nubile-faced young man stood awkwardly next to Johnnie and waited for an introduction. Johnnie inhaled and said, "I want you all to meet the love of my life. This is Calvin."

Everyone shook hands and repeated their names. Mel could not help but stare at Calvin. His natural blonde hair cut in a distinctively feminine page-boy style framed a creamy complexion sans any signs of facial hair. His eyebrows arched perfectly with eyelashes longer than legal. Calvin caught Mel's eye and said in a soft childlike voice, "Johnnie has told me so much about you. It's a real pleasure."

Mel detected an unobtrusive curtsy. They held hands.

"I've yet to get the entire story on how you met, but I'm sure we're going to be longtime friends," Mel said, easing his tension.

They dropped hands, and Calvin reached for Johnnie's arm and clung tight.

"So," Mel said, changing the subject, "What's your wonderful news, Terry?"

Terry looked at Taylor and motioned for him to answer.

"Talked to the D.A. today. Laid it all out . . . everything. And he's agreed not to press the indictment . . . for now."

Everyone cheered.

Taylor patted the air, "Let's not get too comfortable. The

203

D.A. sent the case back to the police department. They'll be digging harder than ever. If there's any chink in Terry's armor, they'll open her up like a can opener."

"That won't happen," Terry said. "I did nothing wrong. I promise all of you that."

"We believe you," Johnnie said.

"Or we wouldn't have taken your case," Mel added.

"What were you accused of, if you don't mind my asking?"

"Murder, Lucas."

Mel felt Lucas' fingers tighten around hers. She leaned toward him and said, "We don't believe Terry murdered anyone. And X-Ray doesn't have any clear evidence on her."

"I don't think I ever met a murderer before," Calvin quietly added.

"And you haven't now," Taylor said.

The disc jockey announced, "This is a night of joy. Let the celebration begin."

As noise thickened the air, Johnnie held Calvin's hand and they ran to the dance floor. An exotic dancer seized Taylor's arm.

"Can you excuse us?" Lucas asked Terry.

Terry waved them off and turned her back to the dance floor.

Taylor and his partner, Johnnie and Calvin, and Mel and Lucas found each other and made a wide circle, dancing with no one and everyone. Mel spun halfway round and stopped mid-step. Her heart pounded at the vision of Terry being kissed by Dr. Reynolds.

Mel excused herself by fanning her face and withdrew, leaving Lucas in the group. She maneuvered through the crowd to the bar and walked up to the small band of women. One woman had her hand propped on Terry's shoulder. Another stood beside Terry.

"Well, hello," Mel said, in a breathless voice.

"Don't be so surprised to see me here, Ms. Walker. Most of the work in this room is mine. And I can't wait to get my hands on you." Dr. Reynolds lightly touched the side of Mel's cheek near her ear and hairline. "I can take ten years off your life. Just like that." She snapped her fingers.

"I thought a Dr. Adams did a lot of plastic surgery in Orange County," Mel tossed out, remembering the dead man in the morgue.

"He certainly does," Dr. Reynolds answered. "He's an excellent surgeon."

"But Sarah is the best. I'm a living testament to that," Terry added, cupping her breasts.

The woman touching Terry leaned in and laughed.

Someone brushed against Mel and she twisted around. "Excuse me," she said, as she stepped back giving herself some distance from the group.

"Hello, gorgeous." A gray-haired stranger extended his right hand. "My name is Irving Goldberg." He handed her a business card.

"Thank you, Mr. Goldberg." Mel turned the card over.

"Please call me Irving."

"Oh, you're a private investigator. So am I."

"Yes, I know."

"Your name sounds familiar, but I don't believe we've ever worked any cases together. Have we?"

"Not yet."

"I didn't mean to be rude. Irving, let me introduce you. This is our host Terry Malone. But you must know her or you wouldn't be here?"

"I might have come with a friend."

"But you didn't?"

"Maybe."

Mel took note of his avoidance and continued introductions to those people she knew. Irving appeared a bit bold and arrogant at first. But as he joined the conversation, her thoughts about him mellowed. Baby-fine curls covered his head. His infectious laugh was hearty and warm. Black, horned-rimmed glasses protected hazel eyes on a handsome face that sported a neatly trimmed, black-and-gray mustache.

The music ended and another fast song began. Johnnie and Calvin worked their way through the crowd and Johnnie hollered, "You can't believe how many of our friends are here tonight. I'm so happy to see everybody."

"These are like my kids," Terry said, motioning to the entire room.

Two women climbed the steps to the stage and stood on either side of a brass railing. The disc jockey's husky voice said, "Clarisse and Jennifer want to perform for you tonight. Please put your hands together and welcome them to the stage."

Soft jazz from a sax began to play. Mel scanned the room, watching as couples paired, whispering, exchanging intimacies. Lovers held hands, others caressed. Lucas made his way from the restroom and joined her. He stood behind her and placed his arms over her shoulders. She looked up at him and whispered, "I know this sounds extremely bizarre given this moment and place in time but . . ."

Lucas anticipated her sentence, "I adore you too."

"That's not what I meant, but hold that thought for later."

"What were you going to say?"

"I just had the most incredible epiphany. Now I just have to prove it."

❖ Chapter 37 ❖

Mel opened the door to her home and stood facing Lucas, her hands behind her.

Lucas leaned forward, his hands above her head. "Into your head," he said, as he turned her head up and kissed her hair gently.

"Would you like to come in?"

"Into your home?" He kissed her forehead.

She took his hand in hers, leading him into the entry hall. They kicked their shoes off and began a slow ascent up the stairs.

"Into your heart." He nibbled the inside of her left breast, as he unbuttoned each button, briefly touched each exposed area with the tip of his nose. Lucas removed her blouse and set it across the railing, then darted his tongue up and down her sternum.

Mel moved her buttocks up one riser at a time toward the top of the stairwell. Her hands moved slowly over his shoulders and arms, hungrily returning his yearnings. Lucas grasped her hands and interlaced their fingers. Their heated bodies touched and fire exploded deep inside her belly.

"Into your soul." His voice slow and determined, Lucas' face dove deep into her stomach, kissing, and moving his tongue over the ripples of her rib cage. She held his head close, encouraging the attention.

"Into your spirit." Lucas unbuttoned the red silk slacks, lifted her hips with one hand, and slipped them down her legs with the other. His mouth lightly rippled across and down each shoulder.

Mel fumbled with his shirt buttons and pulled the shirt off exposing his bronzed arms. His washboard stomach moved urgently in-and-out. She ran her fingers over his body, pausing to count the muscles as she pushed him back to look into his eyes.

They reached the top landing and Mel lay flat against the carpet with Lucas beside her. One of his muscular legs draped over her body. His tongue found the depth of Mel's mouth and she caught her breath.

She murmured, "Do you have any bad habits I should know about?"

"I snore often . . . and loud."

"I don't think you're going to get much sleep tonight."

❖ Chapter 38 ❖

"Good morning, Mel. Good morning, Lucas." Rosa tapped on the closed door. "Breakfast will be ready in less than twenty minutes. Is that okay?"

Mel rolled over and snuggled next to her sleeping giant. "That's fine." She whispered, "Honey?"

"Hmm?"

"We've got twenty minutes."

"I'll hurry." Lucas turned over and enveloped her body in his arms, as the door shot open and slammed against the wall.

"Good morning, loves," Johnnie and Calvin chimed. "Rise and shine."

Mel and Lucas reached for the bedcovers and raised their heads above the linens.

"Give us a break," Mel pleaded.

Johnnie and Calvin ignored them and flung themselves, elbows first, on the end of the bed. Johnnie giggled. "You don't have anything I haven't seen at least once or twice before."

"Don't be too sure," she said, rubbing his belly.

Lucas ducked under the sheets and Mel tickled him into chuckling.

"Rosa's preparing breakfast. Get dressed so we can eat," Johnnie said.

"Can I ask you a personal question first? I mean really personal, Johnnie."

"Shoot."

"You said something curious last night. About seeing lots of your old friends. Did you mean lots of gay guys? And lesbians?"

"Dear Mel. I must say."

"Can you tell me who they are?"

"I'm not going to 'out' anyone. There's an unwritten code. We just don't do that to each other."

"I'm not renting a plane with a banner proclaiming anyone is gay, for God's sake." Mel wrapped the sheet across her breasts and sat cross-legged under the covers. Lucas pushed himself up and did the same.

"It's a gay pride thing . . . not really sworn to . . . like we didn't take a blood oath. It's just something we've always followed," Calvin added.

"What if it concerned a case? Let's say it may be more than pertinent . . . crucial, even," Mel asked.

"Honey, it may not be right to press here," Lucas said.

Johnnie and Calvin nodded in agreement.

"Okay, then, let's play a game. I'll say a name and you nod. Can we at least do that?"

Calvin and Johnnie looked at each other and hunched their shoulders. Johnnie relented first, "Okay, but not to everyone at the party." He held up one finger.

She frowned.

Then two fingers.

"Don't waste them," Lucas said.

"Okay." She stared at the ceiling fan for a moment. "Hmm. Can we agree then, that our client Terry Malone is at least bisexual?"

The exaggerated shock on Johnnie's face gave the answer away. "How would you have guessed that?"

"I'll go you one better. I'm going to guess who one of her lovers is or was?"

Johnnie nudged Calvin and winked. "Lay your money down lady. You'd never guess in a million . . ."

"Dr. Sarah Reynolds," Mel blurted out.

Mel counted three slack-jawed, buggy-eyed men sitting on or lying in her bed.

"Shit," Johnnie said. "You are good."

"Better than that, listen to this scenario. What if . . .?"

Rosa called out from below, "Breakfast is ready."

Mel sat her coffee cup down and pushed her chair back. "Johnnie, I'll need you to pick up the real estate copies I ordered. Can you do it today?" she asked.

"No problem. Where can I find you?"

"At the office. I haven't opened mail in days."

"Calvin and I will drop them by later."

Lucas leaned over and kissed Mel on the head. "Honey, I've got a meeting with my Saudi crew. I'll call you this afternoon."

She stood and hugged him. Rosa waved everyone away from the kitchen and out of the house.

The car phone rang as Mel pulled into the office driveway.

"Mel Walker speaking."

"Hi. What's happening?"

"Good morning Taylor. Just got to the office. Where are you?"

"About twenty minutes away. Can I drop by?"

"Sure. Come on."

Mel sorted through a large stack of mail and returned several calls when she heard a car door slam.

"Come in Taylor," she called out.

"Hi, honey."

He reached for Mel and tried to kiss her. Her arms remained at her side and she turned her head away.

"I'd expect a bigger thanks than this for getting Terry off."

She pushed him away and stepped back. "What are you talking about? I don't owe you anything. You were doing your job. That's what Terry paid you to do."

"You didn't think I was capable of winning. I showed you. I'm entitled to more than a cold shoulder and a reprimand."

"Taylor, you had a duty, a fiduciary responsibility to Terry. And doing the best job you can do won't get you back in my bed." She turned and walked to her office. He followed.

"I did it for you . . . for us."

"You're so misguided. It's far too little and too late."

"It's Lucas, isn't it?"

"Forget who it might be. Who it isn't . . . is you. And never gonna be. Sit down. I have a few questions for you."

He slumped into the sofa and stared at the floor. His jaw clenched.

"Did you know your client was bisexual?"

Taylor made no facial or body movements. He simply replied with his fingers forming a tent as he leaned back on the couch. "Mel, you know anything my client tells me is privileged."

"Okay, you know Terry is bi. And you also know Terry's one-time lover was Peter Connelly, my deceased client. Do you know her one-time lady-lover was Dr. Sarah Reynolds?"

He did not move a muscle. "I'm not blinking first."

"You always did play a mean game of poker with that face. Did you know Terry and Sarah own property in the same subdivision?"

"So?" He stood and walked toward the door, then paused, "I'm all out of answers. But this . . . between us, is far from settled."

"You're such an asshole."

The front door slammed shut and the phone rang.

She grabbed the receiver and angrily answered with "Walker Investigations. Mel Walker speaking."

"Don't be mad at me. I didn't wake you up this morning."

"Hi, X-Ray. Sorry. My asshole ex-husband just slammed out of the office."

"That's who I'm looking for. I'm trying to catch up with him about your discovery."

"Haven't heard from the D.A. yet?"

"No. You wouldn't want to give me a little hint would you?"

"I have a question for you? Why did the police suspect Terry in these murders?"

"First, we knew she deposited large sums of money which she could not or would not explain to us."

"Our investigation report will clear that up for you."

"Right. Number two, the weapon belonged to her."

"Circumstantial. Doesn't mean a thing."

"All right. I don't deny we have some problems. We can't tie Terry, the weapon, and the bodies at the same place and time. We have re-verified her alibis on each incident. Where has your investigation taken you?"

Mel said in a hushed voice, "Did you know Terry and Peter were heterosexual lovers, and Terry and Dr. Sarah Reynolds were lesbian lovers?"

The pause became her answer.

"X?"

"Hmm. I do now. What's someone's sex life got to do with our murders though?"

"I'm not sure if it does at all. Just developing facts and placing each piece of the dynamics on the puzzle board."

"When you see the big picture, get back to me."

"Bye, big guy."

Mel fumbled through the Yellow Pages Directory and located Dr. Reynolds' large ad.

"Hello. This is Marianne Burger with the phone company," Mel said.

"Yes, Miss Burger. May I help you?" the receptionist said.

"We're preparing next year's advertising for Dr. Reynolds. It currently fills one quarter of page 2447. We're wondering if Dr. Adams should be added, or in some way mentioned in this advertisement?" I love fishing expeditions.

"While Dr. Adams does contract work at this location with Dr. Reynolds, perhaps you should speak with his office manager regarding his advertising budget."

"Excellent idea. May I have that number and a name?"

She typed Dr. Adams' number into her reverse telephone program and placed a call to the coroner's office.

"Hi, Sally. This is Mel. Can I ask Barry one question?"

"Hello. Whatcha need lady?"

"Barry, sorry to bother you. Got a question on the pec-lift guy. This is a case I'm helping X-Ray with. You listed a Dr. Adams on the certificate? Can you tell me where his office is?"

"It's a private mail box number. I don't have a physical address on him."

"Who was listed as his attending?"

"Dr. Sarah Reynolds."

"According to their report, where did death occur?"

"Mr. America died in her surgical unit."

"Any chance the body might be a homicide?"

"I found an unusual needle mark."

"Isn't that normal for surgical IV's?"

"The injection site doesn't appear to be part of the intra-muscular medication."

"Please check it out for me . . . for X-Ray," she added.

"Toxicology will take some time. And the guy's ex-wife wants to cremate him as soon as possible."

"Hold him as long as you can. Talk with you later. Bye."

"Later."

The monitor clock ticked away searching for a matching address to Dr. Adams' phone number. Seconds later the number 16255 Thompson, Tustin Hills, California spread across the dotted line.

Mel hit the print key.

Office distractions filled her afternoon. The front door opened and startled Mel.

"Who's that?" she called out.

"Why isn't the door locked?"

"Hi, guys. I'm in my office. It's unlocked because we're open for business."

Johnnie and Calvin entered the room carrying long rubber-banded documents. "With someone following you, I prefer it locked. Business can knock," was Johnnie's response.

"All right. You're such a nag. What's all this?"

"The building department copied every piece of paper they had on the two properties. Cost me a fortune to get them out of hock."

"So, turn in an expense account. Lay them on that chair and I'll go over them later. Guess what? I found out who lives in the home behind Terry."

"Who?"

Mel gave Johnnie the print out. "Dr. Adams. He lives there with another guy. I don't know the other one yet."

"So he certainly knows about the tunnel."

"Yeah."

"Next subject. Do you and Calvin know someone who might have died recently?"

"We lose friends all the time. Anyone in particular?"

"A body builder maybe?"

They looked at each other, frowned, and shook their heads. "Not to our knowledge. Maybe if we had a picture of him we could show it around."

"Drop by Barry's office and get a photo when you have time. No rush."

"Is this the body builder who died after pec lift surgery that you were telling us about?"

"Yeah."

"We'll pick up the photo tomorrow and see what we can develop. In the meantime, got any plans for dinner? You could join Calvin and me."

"Thanks. Yeah. Lucas is supposed to meet me at home about seven. Want to come with us?"

"No thanks. Wanted to make sure you weren't alone. We'll be fine."

"Thank you guys. See you tomorrow."

"But not too early," Calvin said.

The phone rang as Mel watched Johnnie and Calvin climb the stairs to his garage apartment.

"Walker Investigations. Mel Walker speaking."

"I need to see you . . . to talk with you."

"Terry, you sound out of breath. Are you okay?"

The receiver at Terry's end contained background noise that Mel couldn't place. Then the mouthpiece was muffled.

"Terry, are you there?"

"I'm fine." Her voice quivered.

"Is tomorrow soon enough for us to get together? I was just leaving the office for dinner."

"No. No, it isn't. I need you right now. Please come to my home . . . now."

The dialogue sounds scripted, Mel thought.

"Should I bring someone with me?" she said hesitantly, trying for a simple "yes" or "no" answer.

"I have something to tell you and only you. You decide if it needs to go further. Please come. I'm waiting."

Mel beeped Johnnie on the intercom, but he didn't answer. She looked through the blinds. The Mustang wasn't in the driveway. She scribbled a note for Lucas to wait for her and taped it to the computer monitor.

She arrived at Terry's home at sundown and parked at the curb. The two-story Tudor home stood dark and quiet, drapes drawn.

Instinct caused Mel to pull a 9mm from the glove compartment and slip it into her purse before exiting the car.

She walked up the driveway and rang the doorbell. She glanced up and down the street. No one walked their dog, no traffic, no cars parked anywhere. She rang again. Seconds passed.

Hearing no sounds from within the house, she firmly held the doorknob and turned it. The latch clicked and she pushed the door open and stepped across the threshold into a dark entry hallway. Mel detected a shadowy movement from behind the door. She reached for the gun in her purse and fumbled with the clasp. One sharp blow to the side of her head caused Mel to lose consciousness and drop to the marble floor.

❖ Chapter 39 ❖

Each time Mel's rapid heart pounded, a piercing pain shot between her temples. Bright lights added to her discomfort. She dreamed she was conscious.

Someone whispered her name. "Mel, wake up. Wake up. Mel, please. Wake up if you can. I need you."

She turned her face away from the brightness, slowly opened her eyes, and turned toward the plea.

"Here. Open your eyes. Look here. It's me."

She tried to rub her eyes and realized her hands were restrained behind her in the chair. "Where are we, Terry?"

"In a room below the house somewhere, I think."

"In the tunnel?"

"Probably. I've never seen this room before."

The windowless white room had shiny tile floors and lots of chrome fixtures. Terry's legs and wrists were bound by leather straps, as she twisted on what appeared to be an operating table. Three surgical lights focused on her. White and chrome cabinets and countertops lined every wall.

Mel tried to wrench out of the chair and now clearly understood that she, too, was tied to various chair parts with rope.

"Who did this?"

"Adams carried you in. He made me call you. I'm so sorry to

get you in this mess."

"Don't worry about that right now. Why are we here?"

"I guess you're wondering why we're gathered here?" a voice said, as a man opened the steel door and entered the room.

He wore surgical greens and stood well over six feet. He ran long slender fingers through his short blond hair. His bright green eyes drove stakes through Mel's pounding heart.

"Adams?" Mel asked.

He ignored her, as he tied one side of a surgical mask at the back of his neck and gathered shiny chrome instruments from an Autoclave with sterile prongs. He turned on a stereo and music filled the room. He washed his hands in a nearby sink and pulled on plastic gloves.

Mel worked her shoulders back and forth trying to loosen the rope's tension. One hand worked to free the other. She focused on reaching her purse that lay on a nearby stool.

If I can reach my gun, Mel thought.

Terry screamed and worked harder against her own restraints, when she saw the scalpel in Dr. Adams' hand. "What are you going to do?"

"Shut up," he said without emotion.

"Don't panic," Mel said. "I told several people I'd be here."

"Bullshit."

Terry cried and softly sniffled.

"The police are on their way, Terry. We'll be just fine."

"I said shut up."

The door opened and Sarah entered. She, too, wore surgical greens. Paper booties covered her shoes. "Wonderful. You're both awake. Quit slobbering, Terry. It'll be over soon."

"What . . . oh God help me," Terry sobbed as she spotted Sarah's attire.

Sarah opened a cabinet and withdrew a sterile packet of gloves, then washed her hands in the sink.

A phone rang somewhere in the deep recesses of the house beyond the operating room.

"Shit," Sarah said. "Let it ring."

"Mel claims she told the police she was coming here. Better catch it."

Sarah ran from the room leaving the door wide open.

Adams was singing to the loud music, his back turned. Mel scooted the chair until her hands rested against a lower cabinet counter. She tipped the chair's front legs forward and raised her arms, snatching the nearest thing off the counter.

A smooth handle with two sharp sides, she thought.

She turned it upside down and sawed at the ropes on her wrist.

Sarah returned. "That was Detective Ramirez looking for you and your attorney."

"How'd you handle it?" Adams asked.

"Told him Terry and Taylor left for dinner. Didn't know where they were headed."

"Excellent."

Terry's crying became a subdued noise in the room.

"Shit. I almost forgot. Where's her car?" Dr. Adams asked.

"Check the street and the driveway. We should move it. Get the keys out of her purse." Sarah pointed to the stool.

Dr. Adams opened the purse and the keys fell out. "What do we have here?" he said, as he withdrew Mel's gun.

Shit, Mel thought, as her hands continued gnawing until one rope cut through.

"What a delightful new concept," Sarah said.

"How's that?" he asked.

"Instead of both Mel and Terry dying 'under the knife' so to speak, you'll shoot Terry with Mel's gun. And poor Mel will die under anesthesia. So sad, and I liked her so much."

"That makes a lot of sense. I kill someone and take a short commercial break to have plastic surgery?"

"That's not the exact order I have in mind," Sarah said. "Adams, move her car off the street and let's get started."

The whites of Terry's eyes stared in panic as Sarah picked up a hypodermic, filled it, and injected the needle into Terry's arm. Terry struggled against the drug. "Sarah, I love you. How can you do this to me?" Her scream fell silent quickly.

Sarah brushed Terry's hair off her forehead and leaned over and kissed her. "I love you, too. But you've become a liability to me. Sleep my sweet."

Mel spoke, buying time. "I knew about this room and this tunnel, you know."

"Really, tell me about it," Sarah said.

"I drove up here. Talked with neighbors. I knew you and Terry owned property a few blocks from each other. But real estate records indicate an accounting office owns the home directly behind Terry on Thompson Street. I learned that two male doctors live together in that home. One of them is Adams."

"So?"

"Here's the kicker. When I looked at the building department records, there are 1981 permits that place an underground tunnel joining Adams' Thompson Street house to Terry's house on Richelieu. I suspected you . . . maybe you and Adams have lived, or at least stayed at Terry's home at one time or another and used the tunnel to walk between houses and nosy neighbors."

"*Menage à trois?*" Sarah threw her head back and laughed. "Oh-oh. Challenging."

Mel's fingers were raw. She shook but continued to work at the rope, talking all the while. "Terry sent Peter to you, didn't she?"

"Of course."

"And under anesthetic he tells you about the bank's money."

"You are good." Sarah filled the hypodermic again and walked around the operating table toward Mel.

"And you're cunning. A clever physician might move the cash. Then, when Peter and Buddy were released from prison, they were pitted against each other in a struggle to locate the loot."

"It makes such a nice tidy story, doesn't it?"

"Not really. You hired the body builder to murder Peter. That keeps Peter from hiring Johnnie and me. I figure him for the murder of Buddy, too. It'd take someone with his physique to toss Buddy into the flood control channel."

"And?" Sarah smiled and pressed some liquid through the needle that squirted into the air.

"You offer to pay the guy with a free pec-lift, probably in this room, and he accidently dies."

"Ben Franklin said it best, Mel. Something like 'Three can keep a secret if two of them are dead'."

"But three are already dead and now you have Adams, Terry, and me to deal with. Not to mention the entire Harbour Pointe Police Department, if I don't call in soon. You're not going to get away with this."

"You and Terry are among the dead as we speak, dear." Sarah leaned forward and wiped a cotton swab against Mel's bare arm.

"I have a question?"

"What else, for goodness sake? You are a meddlesome bitch." Sarah stood and stepped back two steps.

"I need to know. Was Terry involved in the entire mess, beyond Peter's medical recommendation?"

"She's as innocent as a lamb. I knew from her pillow talk that Peter had big bucks. I suggested that if he wanted some work done, I'd be glad to help."

"I don't understand the gun. Why'd you try to frame Terry with her gun?"

"It was really quite simple. Don't forget, as a patron of the Skin Inn, I knew and had access to the gun. It was always kept behind the bar. I took it and gave it to Mr. World to use."

The last cord on her hands broke free and Mel lunged forward and wildly slashed out at Sarah. Mel tried to stand and dragged the chair with her. The sharp instrument grazed Sarah's arm and she dropped the needle and covered the open wound with her other hand to compress the spurting blood. Sarah ran to a medicine cabinet, threw the doors opened and randomly tossed packages and medicine bottles on the floor.

"Bitch," she screamed. "I'll get you for this."

Mel fell face forward to the hard floor. She gripped the knife, rolled to one side, and worked to free the ropes around her legs.

"I'm looking forward to butchering your face. Where is that acid?"

The music blared. Terry lay in a deep coma. Sarah slapped steri-strips on her lacerated arm, then rummaged through a nearby cabinet looking for the chemical. Mel was closer to the floor than the others. She heard the rumble before she felt it.

❖ Chapter 40 ❖

From deep within the bowels of the earth's core, the ground, like a hungry stomach, boiled to the surface. Vials of fluid shook and toppled over. Cabinet doors rattled. Glasses touching clicked, then cracked.

Dr. Reynolds spun around. An evil smile began at the corner of her mouth. "I love it. You'll be buried alive." She ran from the room laughing.

Pieces of the ceiling hit the floor and the growl grew into a roar.

Mel kicked her legs away from the chair. She raced to Terry and unbuckled the restraints. She shook her shoulders.

"Terry, wake up. Now I need you."

"Uh," was Terry's only comment.

Mel swung Terry's legs off the table and slapped her face several times trying to rouse her. Larger chunks of the ceiling tile fell on and around them. She plopped Terry belly-down on the stool with wheels, clutched two canisters of oxygen and raced through the steel door. The hallway ran in two directions. Mel had no problem deciding which corridor to take. A wall of debris fell blocking one path and columns of dust filled the small area.

Mel pushed the stool, clearing clods of earth and broken pilings and electrical wiring along the way. She then ran a short way back and dragged the canisters of air past her, Terry and the stool. She continued for another twenty feet until she turned a curve and spotted a doorway. The lights failed. The ground vibrated with a hard singular jolt and more walls collapsed around them, making further advance impossible. One larger piece knocked Mel unconscious.

❖ Chapter 41 ❖

The lack of air in her lungs made Mel gasp and wake up. She fumbled in the dark and found one oxygen canister. She brought it to her mouth, turned a knob and inhaled. She groped around until she touched Terry's legs and followed her body to her face; then she placed the mask over Terry's mouth.

She kicked around in a small circle until her feet struck the other canister. She lifted it to her own face and took another breath.

Seconds became minutes. Mel kept occupied by rubbing Terry's legs and arms and talking to her, hoping the touch, with help from the oxygen, would rouse her.

Be calm, she thought. We will be saved.

"X-Ray I'm here," she cried. "Oh, Lucas. Please find us."

Mentally she conjured a picture of a massive rescue in progress above all this rubble. Intellectually she realized the earth might have split with this shelf movement and they might be buried alive along with the entire population of Southern California.

She quit rubbing Terry.

Better that Terry die in her sleep than suffer what's ahead for us, she thought. Mel heard her heart pounding. Sweat dripped across her face and arms, and down the small of her back.

The ground shaking had ceased. Dust particles and debris filled the air. Mel's damp hair stuck to her forehead. She wiped her hair back with raw hands and fingers that stung from the perspiration.

Then, like a tunnel drill on its hands and knees, she tossed dirt away from what she remembered had been the only exit.

She reached the door but it was jammed and wouldn't open. Mel kicked at it. Blood ran down both knees into her shoes.

"That's not gonna work," Terry said.

She ran back to Terry and helped her stand. "I hoped you would sleep through all this."

"And miss all this fun. What the hell happened?"

"The short version? Earthquake. Sarah and Adams ran away. We're buried somewhere in the tunnel, and no one on earth has a fucking idea where we are."

"And the good news is . . .?"

"We're getting low on oxygen."

The two took turns tapping on the metal door with one of Terry's rings. They turned off one oxygen canister and shared the other.

"Terry, do you know Morse Code?"

"I can barely write a letter."

"Me either."

"What are you going to do when we get out of here?"

"I hadn't thought about it."

228

"Marry that fine looking Texan?"

She sighed. "I don't know. Would you marry again?"

"I loved Peter so much. He was a warm and wonderful man. I wish you'd had the chance to really get to know him. Probably not."

Silence.

"What are you thinking?" Mel asked.

"I'm wondering where that noise is coming from."

"What noise? I thought you cleared your throat."

Whiny sounds of grinding engines and vibrations from machines became louder and nearer.

"We're going to be saved, Mel. They're coming for us."

"My concern is the weight and movement will cause the whole thing to fall in on us. Most of your house is above us, isn't it? I just received the copies of the plans today and didn't take a good look at them."

"The tunnel connects my home to Dr. Adams', but I thought it started at my basement door, skirted around the pool and gazebo, then ran under the back fence to his basement door."

"You hadn't seen the operating room before?"

"Sarah told me she had a wine cellar here. But she always kept it locked."

"I wish we had some light. I wonder how much oxygen we have left?"

Dirt and dust continued to rain on them. They used their hands to clear the debris from in front of the jammed door when a voice hollered. "Stand away from the door."

They crouched against a far corner and covered their heads. Several seconds passed. A large thud-like noise struck the door, then the jaws of life gnawed through it like a can opener.

"You ladies okay?" a rescuer called out.

"We're fine. What took you so long?"

❖ Chapter 42 ❖

Over the ringing of the ambulance siren, Mel asked, "How'd you know where to find me?"

"When you didn't meet Lucas for dinner, we knew you were dead or kidnaped," X-Ray said.

"How'd you figure out I'd be here?"

"I don't tell all my secrets." X-Ray leaned over and kissed Mel on the forehead.

"Ouch, that hurts. Actually everything I have aches."

"I'll bet it does. Rest now. We'll talk later."

"Is Terry okay?"

"She's right behind us in another unit."

"Get us a room together," Mel slurred the last word then slept.

They stood like archangels in a wide circle encompassing both hospital beds: X-Ray, Johnnie and Calvin, Lucas, Rosa, and Taylor.

"Are we going to live?" Mel whispered, when she opened her eyes.

"And how," Johnnie said, as he patted her shoulder.

Mel winced, then turned toward Terry who was sitting on her

bed wearing a pink nightgown with a plunging neckline, her assets clearly visible through the material. Terry's feet dangled off the side. She wore matching pink slippers that had large boa puffs on top. "Why do you look so good and I feel like hell?"

"You did the work and I slept through it all." Terry looked in a compact mirror and applied lipstick. Then she scrunched her hair with one hand and laughed. "You look like hell, too." She slid off the bed and padded toward Mel.

"You're wrapped like a mummy. Lots of scrapes, lacerations, and bruises, but no broken bones," X-Ray said.

Terry lifted one of Mel's bandaged hands. "And no finger nails."

"And no skin on either hand or knees," Lucas said.

"And Sarah and Adams?" Mel asked.

"Backhoe found their bodies in the rubble just above the tunnel. Apparently they chose to stay with the house and it collapsed around them," X-Ray said.

"How'd you know where we were?" Mel asked.

Johnnie spoke first. "Remember, I just picked up the plans. We talked about the tunnel and how Dr. Adams was Terry's underground partner."

"We knew someone or something distracted you from meeting Lucas. Since I'm the detective here . . . I came to the office and saw your note to Lucas. Then just like you found out who your client was . . . simply dialed pound 69 to see who called you last," X-Ray said.

"X-Ray called Terry's home and Sarah answered. Told him Terry and Taylor were out to dinner," Johnnie said.

"Taylor was in his office and hadn't talked with Terry at all," X-Ray said.

"How bad was the earthquake?" Mel asked.

"The center was the Newport-Inglewood fault just off the coast. Orange County has lots of rebuilding to do, but the deaths and injuries are minimal," X-Ray said.

"Is there any good news?" Mel wanted to know.

"Barry took tissue from the body builder. The DNA matched it to that found in the car. That'll at least place him in the car with Buddy," X-Ray said.

"Sarah confessed she and Adams hired the body builder to dispose of both Peter and Buddy. Then, they decided to eliminate him during surgery," Mel said.

"Great. That closes three homicides for me."

"And while Terry was out cold, Sarah told me Terry knew nothing about this elaborate plot to steal the money from Peter," Mel said.

Terry began to cry and pulled a tissue from the bed stand. "Thank you so much, Mel. I can't tell you how much that means to me. I've never had anyone believe in me like you folks have. Thank you again for all your support."

Johnnie put his arm around Terry's shoulder. "It was our pleasure, believe me."

"That pretty well wraps everything up doesn't it?" X-Ray said.

"Not quite," Johnnie said. "Who was following us?"

"Irving Goldberg. He tipped his hand at Terry's party. He's a private eye. I suspect Dr. Reynolds hired him to tail us to make sure we weren't getting too close to the truth," Mel said.

"Let the police department handle that. I'll pull him in on some charge and threaten to take away his investigator's license."

233

❖ Chapter 43 ❖

Mel rolled the butcher papers tight and wrapped a rubber-band around them. She bit the cap from the marker pen and wrote,"Paul Connelly's Case," then replaced the top, jamming it tight with her tongue. She set the roll on end against one corner of the storage closet wall and shut the door.

"What's next for us?" Johnnie asked, as he leaned against the office door.

"I'm not very happy about this one yet."

"What do you mean? You couldn't have scripted it any better. Dr. Adams and Dr. Reynolds died after admitting to the three murders. Toxicology reports indicate they injected their patient with a lethal dose of sodium bicarbonate. X-Ray found all the DNA he needs to tie the bodybuilder to both murders . . . and to Dr. Reynolds. Best of all, Terry has been exonerated," Johnnie said.

"No prison time, but she's got lots of taxes and penalties to pay," Mel said.

"Glad I don't have to pay the government any money."

"Whew, me too."

"But at what price for her own freedom? What a shock that must have been to find out the body builder in the morgue was Terry's half-brother. When's the funeral?"

"Taylor told me the body was cremated and there won't be any memorial."

"How's she taking it? Have you talked with her?"

"To find out that Dr. Reynolds killed a family member and plotted the death of her lover was a double-whammy."

"I understand that all too well, Mel. But she's a survivor. She's going to be fine."

"I hope you're right."

Mel walked into the office and plopped down in her chair. Johnnie followed her and lay back on the sofa. She chewed on the eraser end of a pencil and said, "Hmm."

"What is churning up there in that organized, yet muddled brain of yours?"

"I don't know . . . intuition, gut feelings, maybe nothing."

Mel opened a file drawer beside her desk and flipped through several manila folders. She pulled one out and opened it.

The phone rang.

"Walker Investigations, Mel Walker speaking."

"Hi, Mel."

"Hi, X. What's happening?"

"I thought you ought to know. The banks can't trace the cash from their serial numbers on that robbery."

"That's too bad. But you were able to prove Dr. Reynolds had a cash infusion that matched that amount, didn't you?"

"Yes. Those funds, less a few thousand that I suspect Peter Connelly spent on getting his surgery and other personal needs, can't be accounted for. No problems so far."

"That's wonderful."

"There's more great news."

"What?"

"The bond. The bond was not part of the heist. Terry sent me

235

a receipt showing she purchased it and gave half to Peter so he could hire you. She has the other half. The fee is all yours. Free and clear. Except for the taxes you'll have on the income, of course."

"It was all about money, wasn't it?"

"Yeah."

"I'm so glad I didn't have that surgery. I could have been victim number four."

"That's a chilling thought."

"You're pretty satisfied that's all we need to wrap up this case?"

"Nice and tidy. Many thanks to you and Johnnie. Say, there is one other question . . ."

"Can you hold? I have another call coming in."

"I'll call you later," X-Ray said.

"Walker Investigations. Mel speaking."

"Hi, hon."

"Hi, Taylor."

"I wanted to thank you for all your work on Terry's behalf."

"No problem, and you're welcome. I was happy to help."

Johnnie nodded and whispered, "Tell him, me too."

"What? Is someone there with you?"

"Yeah. Johnnie said he's glad too. We like Terry a lot."

"Another reason I called was to invite you and Johnnie to the Skin Inn. Terry wants to thank you in person. She and I hope you can come."

"When?"

"Saturday night. Is Lucas still here?"

"No. He left this morning."

"Good. I was hoping to spend some time alone with you."

"Alone? A topless night club is not alone, Taylor."

"It's a start. We can use a fresh beginning."

"I'll meet you there. I have some appointments earlier, so I don't know where I'll be before the revelry begins."

"Can I bring Calvin?" Johnnie called out.

"Yeah. Tell Johnnie, Calvin is a keeper and he's invited too."

Saturday morning began with a deep, marine-layer of fog blanketing the coastline. A gray, oily mist rolled ashore and hung heavily, clinging to everything.

Mel sat cross-legged on the living room carpet, a coffee cup in hand, and twisted the ends of her hair over her ears. She stared at the spot on the horizon where Santa Catalina would be, if she could see it. She sighed, as Vangelis filled the empty house with keyboard, synthesizer, and awkward harmonic sounds.

The phone rang and she let the recorder catch it.

"Hey, Mel. If you're there, pick-up," X-Ray called to her.

She rolled onto her stomach, propped her elbows on the carpet, and picked up the hands-free phone.

"Can't I have a few minutes peace this weekend?"

"We need to talk."

"What about?"

"It isn't over, is it?"

"No."

"Can I drop by?"

"I guess so. Where are you?"

"Parked at the curb in front of your house."

Mel padded to the door barefoot, then returned to the floor, and leaned against the couch. "What do you want from me?"

"I want to see your eyes," X-Ray replied, as he poured a cup of coffee from the kitchen and joined her on the carpet.

"You what?"

"Your dad always said, 'Mel has police eyes'."

"So?"

"You have excellent instincts. There's something else nagging you, isn't there?"

"I have some loose ends, that's all." Mel avoided direct eye contact.

"Right." X-Ray rested against the back of the couch, laid his hand over hers, and listened.

❖ Chapter 44 ❖

Mel had no trouble persuading X-Ray to drive her to the Skin Inn.

"Even when I walked a beat, I never saw the inside of a topless bar," he had replied, smiling.

X-Ray stood behind Mel in line at the entrance. Bouncers asked each person for their name, checked it against a clipboard, and pulled back the curtain.

"I wasn't invited," X-Ray whispered to Mel.

"You're my escort. Not to worry."

"Your name, please?" the door checker asked when they reached the front of the line.

"Mel Walker."

A large black man glanced at his board, made a mark on the paper, then looked up. "Oh, hi, Detective Ramirez."

X-Ray extended his right hand. "You look familiar."

"You busted me once."

"Assault. I remember now. Name escapes me."

"Just call me Bro. And I'll call you sir. Deal?" He stood feet wide apart and smiled, exposing a gold front tooth.

The man stood so tall he barely cleared the door header and his girth filled the width of one of the double doors. With a perfectly round bald head and a single gold ring in his right ear, he reminded Mel of someone.

Mr. Clean, she thought.

Buffet tables covered with food platters lined two walls.

"Hmm. Smells like chicken," Mel said.

"There's roast beef, one of my favorites. Want a drink first?"

"Anything without alcohol or caffeine. I'll find our group."

"I'll catch up with you."

Someone touched her elbow and she smelled a fragrance she knew too well. "Hi, Taylor."

"You brought X-Ray?"

"He had nothing to do tonight. It's his victory too."

Taylor took Mel's arm and led her through the throng to the bar. They cut between two people in the food line. He said, "Follow me. Terry and Johnnie are waiting for you."

The ever ebullient Terry wore a flesh-colored jumpsuit. While her hair covered part of her shoulders, it did nothing to hide the fact she wore no bra.

Terry opened her arms and hugged Mel.

Mel whispered in Terry's ear, "How are you, really?"

"I'm fine," Terry's alcoholic breath whispered back. "And you?"

"Me, too. Bandages are gone." Mel turned the palms of her hands up, then over.

"No nails yet. I'll give you my manicurist's phone number."

"No thank you. I'm not keen on referrals right now."

They all laughed.

"You are one exotic creature," Mel said, feeling blood rushing to her face.

Terry spun around making her hair whirl. "You like?"

"It's very daring."

"My dear, you have a beautiful body too. You need to learn to

240

be comfortable with yourself."

Mel wore a black-linen sheath under a black three-quarter-length jacket. She held the coat edges and brought them around her frame, buttoned one hole, then replied, "I'm very comfortable, thank you."

The group unleashed a nervous chuckle.

"Wow," was all X-Ray could say when he saw Terry.

Terry stepped forward and pressed herself against X-Ray in an embrace. Mel took her drink from his hand as the liquid sloshed to the rim of the glass.

"If you'll excuse me, I see someone . . ." Mel left the circle.

"Well, if it isn't Irving Goldberg."

Goldberg wore a high-necked, black silk shirt and slacks, carried an empty glass and a small platter with food scraps. He turned left, then right, looking for a place to set them down. A waiter appeared and took them from him.

"Hi," Irving said. He wiped his hands on a napkin, then offered his right hand.

"Good to see you. I think we have something to talk about."

"We do?"

"I know you've been tailing me."

"Me?"

"Don't try to deny it. I dropped by your office this morning. Your secretary was kind enough to show me your lovely collection of license plates."

"No crime there. I collect them. Got 'em from every state in the union."

"Especially fond of Arizona and Colorado, aren't you?"

"Not particularly."

"I hope you got what you were looking for. Regardless, I want it to stop." Mel jabbed her finger into his shirt.

"Tailing is better than stalking. And there's nothing illegal about tailing. It's what we do, you and me."

"Don't even try to compare your work to mine. Get this. Nobody tails me." Mel's lips turned up on one side of her mouth.

"You shouldn't be bothered again."

"I won't be bothered again. I just need to know just one more thing."

"What's that?"

"Sarah Reynolds hired you to follow me, didn't she?"

"Two of my favorite private eyes, hanging together and chatting. I like that," Taylor said, as he approached Mel and Goldberg. "Please excuse us, Irving."

The private investigator called to someone in the crowd and left.

"I think we have a lot to talk about, Taylor," Mel said.

"Baby, I'm so glad to hear you say that."

Taylor wrapped his arm around Mel and nuzzled the top of her head.

She pushed him away. "That's not what I meant."

"Wha . . .?"

"You are dirty, Taylor. I don't know exactly how or when, but you're in this somehow."

He gave her one of his poker faces and held back a smirk. "Honey, you've always had a vivid imagination. I get one criminal case and zap, you have me all tangled up in a triple murder." He pursed his lips and squeezed his eyebrows.

"I want the truth. I thought Sarah hired Irving to tail me.

Now I'm thinking it was you."

"Now honey, this isn't the time, nor the place." He straightened his back and sighed.

"This is exactly the right place and time. I'm going to tell you a story. Try this scenario for size. You hired Irving to tail Johnnie and me, thinking that we were getting close. You wanted to know who we saw, where we went, and who we talked with."

Taylor looked at his feet, shuffled at the floor, and shook his head. "Why would I do that, Mel? I hired you. Remember? I knew everything you did because you reported to me."

"Because, I believe . . . and this is where it gets a little confusing . . . you and Terry are now having, or had an affair."

"What are you saying. I love you. I've always loved you."

"I'll put my share of our fee from this case on the possibility that you and Sarah Reynolds were the original lovers in this triangle . . . not Dr. Reynolds and Dr. Adams. And not Dr. Reynolds and Terry. Although I may never be able to prove it, you and Sarah may have set up this elaborate scheme to steal Peter's money. You tried to frame Terry for it. And it looks like you've dumped Terry now that you've achieved your goals."

"What goals are those?" Terry asked, as she joined the circle.

"Sarah, Adams and maybe Taylor. They got Peter's money, didn't they?" Mel asked the small group.

"What are you talking about? Mind you, I'm not admitting anything. Since when is making love against the law."

"It is . . . if you're the mastermind behind stealing Peter's money and framing Terry for murder."

"Semantics, honey. Who cares where the bucks are? Remember, the dough wasn't his anyway. He stole it from a bank."

"But Johnnie was shot and three men lost their lives over this

243

robbery. What do you call that?"

"Really bad luck."

"That isn't funny," said Mel.

"Hon, I didn't mean it that way. Life is very unpredictable. You never know where a path will lead ya."

"In this case, I'll know. Taylor, I'm going to open your life like gutting a beached whale. I'm going to find out where you got the money to set up that second office in Newport Beach. I want to know how you came to represent Terry in the first place. How the gold chain I bought you when you graduated law school came to be worn around Sarah Reynolds' neck."

The music had stopped. Mel's voice rose above the others in the crowded room. X-Ray, Terry, Johnnie, and Calvin closed ranks around her.

"What is she ranting about? You know how these ex-wives are? She never forgave me for walking out on her."

Terry lashed out, "You didn't use me, did you Taylor? You didn't pretend to care about me, then set me up so my sweet fellow could be killed? Oh, God forgive me. How could I have been so naive? Mel, do you know where Taylor lives?"

"I do now. He's the other man who lived with Dr. Adams on Thompson Street."

"Yes. Thank God I can finally tell you." Terry laid her face in both hands and sobbed. "I swear, Mel. I never meant to make love to Sarah. This was all a terrible mistake. It never happened again. I always loved Peter. Then you seduced me. Taylor, please tell me you didn't betray me?" Terry screamed.

"Answer their questions. We're waiting," X-Ray said.

"I'm not going to discuss anything right now," Taylor's voice quivered. Sweat beaded across his brow.

"Mel, you are so right about all this. I'm so sorry," Terry cried

244

out, as she lunged forward and viciously slapped Taylor across the face several times.

Taylor bolted away from the group and shoved himself through the tight crowd that had gathered. "Let me pass," he screamed, as he headed for the front door, knocking several people down in the process.

"Hold him Bro," Mel screamed to the bouncer at the door.

Epilogue

"I'm sick. Leave me alone," Mel moaned.

"No, you're not ill. Just a confusing affair of the heart, I think," Rosa answered. "I fixed you some tea. Drink this and you'll feel better."

She sat beside Mel on the bed and held a tray on her lap.

"No, I won't feel any better."

"I never liked Taylor, even when you two got married. He's not good enough for you."

"I liked him. Respected him. Even loved him . . . once."

"What's going to happen to him? Is he going to jail?"

"I sure hope so. He had an affair with a client and, although improper, it isn't illegal. That's not what will hang him."

"The murders? You think he knew Sarah Reynolds and Dr. Adams were going to commit a crime?"

"Yeah, I do. That's another issue. Knowledge, including murder, gained by the relationship with Terry is attorney-client privilege. And I'm not sure if he's under any legal obligation to report it. However, his complicity in the cover-up and participation in the murders of Peter, Buddy, and Mr. America place him square in the middle of it. I'd like for him to burn in hell for what he did to everyone. X-Ray is working to tie him in as a co-conspirator. He says he's developed a great case against Taylor. Let's hope the grand jury agrees next week."

"Will he also lose his license to practice law?"

"He should. But maybe not. Someone has to complain to the

bar association first; then there's a hearing. And they're lawyers policing lawyers. I know an attorney in San Diego who murdered someone, served time in prison, and still practices law. The bar doesn't seem to care. No one cares. How could I have been so wrong about another human being?"

"Oh, we're all wrong about things at some time or another in our lives," Johnnie walked into the room carrying a large brown box.

"We are?" Mel rolled over and sat up with a pillow propped against her head and back. She wiped her tears with an edge of sheet.

"Like call him Scat, for instance," Johnnie smiled.

"You found him? That's wonderful."

"Scat came home and brought us some presents."

"And we gonna have to give Scat another name," Rosa said, also grinning.

"Why?"

Johnnie came around the bed and laid the open carton on Mel's lap.

"Like a good female name for a Mama Cat."

Mel leaned over and looked inside the box. Scat lay on her side, licking one of her paws, as six black-and-white kittens vigorously fought for nursing rights at her table.

248

❖ About the Author ❖

Does Joyce look like a PI to you? Maybe it's those late night stakeouts, being shot at, and bombed out–that's beginning to show.

Considered the "Hart-to-Hart" of Southern California investigators, Joyce and her husband Harold investigated cases involving movie stars, mobsters, and millionaires during their careers that spanned several decades. Changes in law enforcement, the judicial system, and how citizens respond, have become bountiful fruit for her *Harbour Pointe Mystery Series*; fictionalized stories taken from her actual case files.

The 1998 debut novel, *The Cop was White as Snow* focuses on the death of a police officer, protagonist Camellia (Mel) Walker's dad. The veteran cop would tell his daughter, "The cop's gone CADS." The nemonic spells out–Corruption, Alcohol, Drugs, and Suicide. But Mel knows he wasn't a dirty cop, and wouldn't commit suicide. The police department disagrees.

In the second novel for this series, *I'm Okay, You're Dead*, protagonist Camellia (Mel) Walker and her associate Johnnie Blake dodge bullets as their new client is murdered. More bodies fall. Why should Mel care about the lives of a couple of ex-cons? Because she's a PI with murders to solve, a quarter of a million dollars to locate, and a powerful sense of right and wrong. A Spring 2000 publication date is scheduled.

With her MBA in hand, no working on her Doctorate, Joyce has written a "How-to" for writers who desperately seek fresh, effective marketing and promotional ideas. *Power Marketing Your Novel* with a January 2000 publication date.

Her experiences with serial killers have led her to the dark world of True Crime/Biography in her upcoming–*The Cross Country Killer, The Glen Rogers Story*. Glen has been given two death sentences; one in Florida and another in California. There are more charges pending. The body count could be seventy. The numbers may include Ron and Nicole.

By the way, did you see the PBS special, *Money Matters* hosted by Jack Gallagher which spotlighted Joyce and Harold?

Check out the Website: http://members@aol.com/jspizer for appearances near you.